don,

To
chou ore Ray Wm.

Copyright © 2017 Ray Wenck
Editor: Jodi McDermitt
Cover: Tyler Bertrand
Published by Glory Days Press

All rights reserved. Except as permitted under U. S. Copyright Act of 1976, no part of this publication may be reproduced, distributed or transmitted in any form or by any means, or stored in a database or retrieval system, without prior written permission of the publisher. This book is a work of fiction. While references may be made to actual places or events, the names, characters, incidents, and locations within are from the author's imagination and are not a resemblance to actual living or dead persons, businesses or events. Any similarity is coincidental.

Acknowledgments

The idea for this book came about from all the readers who stopped by my booth at the many shows I do and asked if *Random Survival* was a choose your own adventure book. At first, I didn't see the connection, but then realized the tag line for Random Survival was, *If the world as you know it ended today, how would you survive?* Many took the question as if they had a choice in the storyline.

So many of you asked that I decided to write an adult version of the books we loved as kids. I thought it would be a fun write and bring back memories of books from my past. I was wrong. It was a difficult book to do. The paths and logistics of keeping them in line proved to be so overwhelming, I almost quit.

I got it to a point where my eyes crossed, then passed it to my editor, Jodi. Jodi warriored through it and sent it back, asking what the heck I was thinking. I had no answer. I had to do a spreadsheet and flow chart to make it work.

Finally, we got it. I hope you enjoy it, but if you want another, you better spread the word, 'cause the only way I'm doing another is if it sells so well, I have no choice.

You'll note that I left the gender and name up to you. I gave a suggestion if you don't want the main character to be you. Follow whichever way you want. That's the idea of the book: to allow you to choose. Also, you'll find a list of survival items at the back of the book. I made it fairly basic so you can add to it as you see fit.

Enjoy the ride. Hope you survive. See if you can make it through in one try. If not, you can either:

A) throw the book in anger.
B) complain the book cheated.
C) give it to a six-year-old to show you how it's done.
D) suck it up and try again.

Other titles by Ray Wenck

The Danny Roth Suspense Series
Teammates
Teamwork
Home Team
Stealing Home
Group Therapy

The Random Survival Post-Apocalyptic Series
Random Survival
The Long Search for Home
The Endless Struggle
Hanging On

Stand-alone Titles
Warriors of the Court
Live to Die Again
Ghost of a Chance
Tower of the Dead

Ray Wenck taught elementary school for 35 years. He was also the chef/owner of DeSimone's Italian Restaurant for more than 25 years. After retiring, he was a lead cook for Hollywood Casinos and the kitchen manager for the Toledo Mud Hens AAA baseball team. Now, he spends most of his time writing, doing book tours, and meeting old and new fans and friends around the country.

Ray is the author of thirteen novels, including the post-apocalyptic *Random Survival* series, the paranormal thriller *Ghost of a Chance,* and the mystery/suspense Danny Roth series. Find a full title list, tour schedule, and more at raywenck.com.

His hobbies include reading, hiking, cooking, baseball, and playing the harmonica.

Pick-A-Path Apocalypse

You stand, leaning on a shovel, looking down at the graves of your spouse and youngest son. Though heartbroken, no tears fall. You are cried out, and no amount of grief can make the tears come.

Once again, you look heavenward and ask the same questions. "Why, God? Why me? Why are they dead? Why couldn't you take me instead?" As before, there is no reply.

Glancing around the yard, you see the grass needs to be mowed, but why? The world has ended; everyone is dead…everyone but you, at least as far as you know. The only time you left your house was to rush your spouse and child to the hospital, but the roads were jammed with others just like you.

For long hours, you struggled to find a way through. Your car was attacked by people just as desperate as you. Bodies lie abandoned everywhere; in cars, along the sidewalks, on the streets. It was hopeless, trying to find medical help. Some of the last few words your spouse says to you are, "Take us home. We'll die in peace." You did, and they did, and now you are alone to face—what? Was death still reaching for you? Was your survival a cruel tease, life to be stripped from you at the last second? And what if it was? Did it really matter anymore?

You slam the shovel blade first into the ground and back away. What to do? What to do? Do you:

1A) give up? Page 6

1B) search for survivors? Page 14

1C) collect items you might need to stay alive? Page 77

1A) Seriously? You give up? You chicken shit! After you're one of the last remaining survivors? Okay. You go into your house and:

1A1) pick up your gun and do the deed fast. Page 7

1A2) take the even more cowardly way out and swallow pills. Page 8

1A3) take the lazy way and go lie down. Page 11

1A1) BANG! You're dead. End of story. Thanks for playing.

1A2) You go to the medicine cabinet and search for something that will work slowly and with no pain. You find a half full bottle of sleeping pills. You take a long swig from a bottle of warm beer, then go into the bedroom.

You lie down on the bed and stare at a photo of last year's family vacation. You were sitting together on the deck of a log cabin overlooking the Smoky Mountains. The smiles are big. The trip and the memory, both happy.

A single tear tracks down your face. You wish you were back there now.

The memories flood your mind as you swallow the first two pills. Over the next five minutes, you finish the pills and polish off the beer. You set the beer bottle down and make yourself comfortable on the pillow. It doesn't take long for a fuzziness to blur your eyes. As sleep takes a firmer grip, an uneasiness grows. Your brain's natural survival instinct sends urgent messages to your body.

"Get up! Move!" it screams at you, but you are slipping deeper into dreamland. Still, the anxiety has taken root. Fear causes an adrenaline spike. You feel roused from your goal. You are at the point of no return. Do you:

1A2a) push the fear aside? Page 9

1A2b) push through the pill-induced haze? Page 10

1A2a) You force yourself to let go and drift into a deep sleep from which you will never wake. You die, but not peacefully. You are haunted by your spouse and son for giving up. Your last moments are filled with vivid nightmares. And you deserve it, chicken shit. Give this book to someone who has a better survival instinct and some common sense.

End

1A2b) Reaching desperately for an image of your spouse who is just out of reach, you scream for her, but she doesn't wait. Instead, she rises higher and higher until you realize you are sitting up in bed, feeling very drowsy. It would be easy for you to lie back down and let the sleeping pills finish their job, but your spouse calls your name. "Larry!" (or insert your name here)

You are now more alert. You realize your desire to live is stronger than you thought. You force your legs over the bed, slump to the floor and stick your fingers down your throat. You spew up what is left of the undigested pills in your stomach.

You stand, but feel woozy, steadying yourself on the bed for balance. For the next hour, you force yourself to walk around the house to wear off the effects of the sleeping pills. You fall several times. Each time, you want to give up, but you hear your spouse calling your name again.

"I'm coming," you say, struggling to your feet. "Where are you?" You search in vain, but after another hour, you no longer feel the pull toward sleep. You still feel groggy, but you are more aware.

In the kitchen, you down a bottle of water. Leaning against a counter, you stare out the window at the two graves. "Thank you, my love, for saving me."

You're still a chicken shit, but you will live to die another day.

Now, go back to the beginning and make a different choice. Don't even think about picking the same one or you die immediately, and the words will disappear from these pages. No, don't look, dummy; you'll be dead. Of course, the words will disappear.

Oh, and don't forget to go back in and clean up the puke.

End

1A3) Depressed, you go into the house and climb the stairs to your bedroom. You stare at the bed you shared with your spouse and feel the pull. You lie down. One hand caresses the empty space next to you. The sorrow builds until you can't stand the pain anymore. You want to die, too.

You stay in bed all day and night, dozing on and off. During the awake times, you recall the best moments of your life. They bring comfort.

By morning, you feel drained and even more tired. Your stomach rumbles, calling for food. You sleep, but fitfully and for short periods. For most of the day, you toss and turn, no longer able to find a comfortable position.

The next morning, you realize you must make a choice. To continue like this requires willpower. You have no motivation to get up, but lying in bed is becoming more difficult. Whatever you decide will take a Herculean effort. You decide:

1A3a) to continue on your path. Page 12

1A3b) to get up and face life. Page 13

1A3a) Though it's difficult, you force all thoughts from your mind other than those of your family. The hardest part is ignoring the now-constant grumbling of your stomach. You make it into the night, growing ever weaker. You're no longer as interested in food. An urge to urinate comes. You do not want to get up, so you roll to the edge of the bed and relieve yourself.

The fourth day brings an endless thirst. You think getting up for a small drink won't change your plans, but you are having doubts and don't want to risk what getting up will do to your resolve.

By nightfall, the periods of sleep far outlast those spent awake, and your thoughts are muddled during times of consciousness. You dream now more than remember.

On the fifth day, you want to get up, but you can no longer summon the energy to do so. Your mind is clouded and you can no longer differentiate between the real and the surreal. Dreams alternate between joyful and nightmarish. Memories are all you have left. You drift deeper and deeper into a relaxed sleep until even the memories cease.

End

1A3b) By the second day, the need for food, drink, and the bathroom make it difficult to focus on your depression. You toss and turn, and although you have no desire to live, you crave water, a sandwich, and the almost sexual sensation of bladder release.

You decide it won't change anything if you get up. You can always lie down again to resume your slow-motion suicide. To convince yourself you are only pausing your plan, after using the bathroom, you fix a peanut butter sandwich, grab a warm beer, and sit in bed while you consume it. You feel energized. Your thoughts turn from your family to your own survival.

After finishing, you scoot down in the bed and try to find a comfortable position. After several hours, you give up and go downstairs. You sit at the kitchen table and stare out the patio doors. The graves are just in view. You choke back a lump in your throat and wonder, *is this what they would want me to do?* The answer is easy, if not a cheat. No, but you don't want to die, either.

You make another sandwich and drink another warm beer.

"Well, if you're gonna do this, you best get started," you say.

Go back to the beginning and choose B or C.

1B) You wander through the streets of your neighborhood, hoping to find another survivor. You can't come to grips with the notion of being the last one on earth. It's unfathomable…however, so was the strange sickness that killed off the population.

Again, you wonder why you survived. Was it dumb luck, or some medical anomaly in your body that made you immune? You may never know, but you might as well try to ensure your survival continues.

Stopping at an intersection, you do a slow three-sixty turn, scanning down each block. You see no one. Nothing is moving. Frustrated, you decide you need a better plan. Do you:

1B1) continue wandering the streets in hopes of finding someone? Page 15

1B2) head toward town? Page 58

1B1) The only two exits from the subdivision are north and south, and many of the streets end in courts, so you decide to walk the neighborhood. You head south, pausing at every house.

You look for movement at the windows, in the side yards and backyards, and in the vehicles. It is time consuming. At the first intersection, a cul de sac, you turn right and follow the curb all the way around until you are back on the main street. There, you turn right and head.

You continue for several hours, looking at every house before moving on. At the last court before swinging north, you see movement at the far end of the street. At first, you're not sure what it is, but you're so excited about finding a sign of life, you're halfway down the block before you realize it's a pack of dogs.

Curious about their odd behavior, you stop. They appear to be ripping at something on the ground. No...several somethings. Then, with gut-wrenching clarity, you understand. The dogs are rending the flesh from two bodies.

God, I hope they were dead before they became dog food.

As you watch, several in the assorted breed pack snap at each other. Even from where you are, you can see the blood-soaked muzzles. They appear extremely aggressive; perhaps a little mad. Still, you wonder if any of them could be a pet. At least then, you wouldn't feel so alone.

The question is answered as one notices you and emits a low, threatening growl. One by one, heads turn; all eyes are focused on you.

"Oh boy!" you say, trying to swallow, but finding it difficult. "Nice dogs. Good dogs. I'm not here to hurt you. I'm your friend." You wish you had some food to offer them, and then realize you already do—your flesh. Do you:

1B1a) advance cautiously and try to make friends? Page 16

1B1b) show you're no threat & back away slowly? Page 55

1B1c) run for shelter? Page 54

1B1a) You move forward, hands out to your sides to appear nonthreatening. As you approach, you keep up a constant monologue with a soft voice and high enthusiasm. You are encouraged to see they all wear collars. They were once someone's pets and could be again. They just need to feel some kindness.

The group of eleven dogs all turn to face you with teeth bared, fur standing on end; a chorus of growls tells you of your mistake.

Too late you see your folly. These dogs are now feral and won't be returning to pet status. A golden retriever barks and snaps its bloody maw, and you know it's time to run. Slowly you back away, and the pack senses your fear. You start to run seconds before they do. It is a race you know you cannot win.

Your mind whirls, searching for an avenue of escape or a safe place. Do you:

1B1a1) veer toward a house? Page 17

1B1a2) head for a parked car? Page 45

1B1a3) keep running? Page 54

1B1a1) You head for the nearest house. It has a fenced yard and a long porch with a white spindled banister. You have seconds to decide. Do you:

1B1a1a) run for the porch? Page 18

1B1a1b) try for the backyard? Page 44

1B1a1a) & 1B1b1) You race across the grass, the dogs closing fast. Leaping the steps, you land on the porch and pull on the storm door. To your relief, it opens; however, the inner door is locked. In desperation, you pound on it, praying someone will open it and save you. You are wasting precious time.

As you turn to flee, the dogs meet you on the porch. You kick violently, sending one airborne and onto the grass as another nips your leg. You swing your arms wildly and kick to clear a path. You feel like you're batting at an angry swarm of bees, except these bees are giant and have large teeth. You are bitten repeatedly. One jumps up on you, and you knock it aside with a vicious cuff to the head.

You take the narrow opportunity for escape and run along the porch. The dogs continue their pursuit. You scream as a Jack Russell Terrier rips a hunk of flesh from your leg. Reaching the banister, you swing your legs over and land in the bushes. The branches scrape at your torn skin, but you power through the pain and gather your strength as you run for the backyard.

The railing is too tall for any of the dogs to leap, and the pack is forced to go back the way they came, giving you time to reach the fence. You are weak and in pain, bleeding from a multitude of wounds, but you manage to unlatch the gate and run through, pulling it closed behind you before the dogs arrive.

You latch it and back away, breathing hard as the dogs jump at the fence and bark. Several try to climb the split rails and the fencing. To your horror, you see a few are close to making it. Still others are trying to dig under the fencing.

You swing around, searching for a safe place or a weapon. A brown log cabin-style shed with a porch sits near the far back corner of the yard. Now that you have a few moments to think, you have several options. Do you:

1B1a1b1) go to the shed? Page 19

1B1a1b2) try to get into the house? Page 24

1B1a1b3) hop the far side fence and make another run for it? Page 28

1B1a1b1) You run toward the shed, only to discover a combination lock through the handles on the double doors. You curse and give the lock a tug, but you understand at once that you will not be getting in that way.

You glance back and see a German shepherd at the top of the fence. It is close to getting over. *Well, better to face one at a time than the entire pack*, you think. But still, you need a weapon.

As you step off the shed's porch, you kick a decorative stone. You bend and pick it up, having a sense of confidence with it in your hand. It's the size of a standard brick, but kidney-shaped and heavier. The shepherd balances on top of the fence and flops over, landing on its back. It is stunned for a moment, and you have an idea.

You move to the side of the shed and smash the window with the rock. Rubbing it along the frame to loosen any attached glass, you toss the rock inside the shed, grab the frame on each side and hoist yourself up. A shard pierces your hand. You wince and ignore it.

You reach inside and snag a two-by-four wall stud to give yourself more leverage, and pull your body through the window just as the shepherd jumps at your legs and snatches your pants. You kick frantically and hear the fabric rip. Then you fall, land painfully on top of a riding lawn mower and roll to the floor. You sit there, astonished to be alive, and feel the throbbing and burning of each abrasion simultaneously.

Stripping off your shirt, you press it to the worst of your wounds. You have two bad bites on your legs, one of which is missing a small chunk of meat. You tear the shirt and wrap the fabric around the wounds as tightly as you can. A few of the scratches are still seeping, but the worst is where you sliced your hand on the glass. You find a rag on a bench and press the cleanest part against the cut.

Sitting on the mower, you catch your breath and relax. You're safe for the moment, but you know you need to clean the wounds as soon as you can or risk infection. With no more doctors around, an infection is a death sentence.

Taking stock of the shed, you find the usual lawn tools: rakes, shovels, a hose, a gas-powered weed whacker, a blower, an edger, and a push mower to go along with the riding mower.

The short workbench and pegboard above it holds an assortment of tools. There is a hammer, screwdrivers of multiple sizes, a ratchet set, pliers, and boxes of nails and screws. You sit and plot your next move. You can strike with the hammer and stab with a screwdriver. You slide both tools in your belt and pick up the weed whacker. You hear a sloshing sound and realize there is gas in the tank. Looking around, you find a gas can with some still inside. You fill up the week whacker's tank and try to start it. After several attempts, it whines into motion.

You look out the window and see the shepherd snarling back at you. It leaps, putting its front paws on the side of the shed. Its face is at least a foot below the window, so you really aren't worried about being bitten. It barks, growls, and snaps, but it can't get to you.

You stick the idling weed whacker out the window and the dog races away. It stands a few feet back, snarling at you. When you pull the weed whacker in, the dog runs forward and places its paws against the shed. You try twice more, but each time the shepherd scampers to safety.

You look around the yard and see several of the dogs are burrowing under the fence. It won't be long until they'll enter the yard. You need to do something now.

You grab the hammer from the pegboard and turn off the weed whacker while you wait for the shepherd to return. This time, when you put your arm out the window and hold the hammer, the shepherd flinches at the sight, but doesn't run away. The sound of the motor running does not startle it.

You hesitate. The thought of injuring a dog makes you nauseous, but you convince yourself it is either the dog or you. Besides, it didn't hesitate to rip open your flesh. You raise the hammer higher and bring it down as hard as you can. The dog jumps down, but not in enough time to miss a solid blow to the side of the head. It yelps and staggers several steps before collapsing.

Adrenaline coursing, you know you have little time. You climb out and reach back inside for the weed whacker, but it isn't within reach. A sound behind you draws your attention. The Jack Russell is the yard and is running at you. The shepherd is now sitting up, still dazed, but trying to clear its head. Two more dogs are coming under the fence where the Jack Russell dug the hole.

With fresh panic, you race for the house. You leap onto the deck toward the patio door with the Jack Russell close on your heels. You whirl, flailing wildly with the hammer. It strikes the dog's flank, sending it yelping and falling to the side.

Turning your attention to the door, you break the glass with the hammer and smash as many shards away as you can. You step through as carefully as the urgency of the situation allows. You hear the Jack Russell's nails scratch on the glass at the bottom of the door. You look out and see not only the terrier, but the shepherd and the golden retriever racing your way.

With a backhand slash, you hit the glass at the head height of the Jack Russell, crashing through and sending the dog flipping over backward. Then, you upend the kitchen table, pressing it against the broken door and blocking the way.

The dogs hit the table and bark ferociously, but you hold it in place and the animals are unable to gain entry. Exhausted, you slide to the floor. For the moment, you are safe.

***

You rest for a long while. The wounds burn and need attention. You get up and grab chairs and tables from the family room and put them in front of the kitchen table to ensure the dogs will not be able to push their way in. Once you feel secure, you rummage through the house in search of medical supplies. You find a box of band-aids and three gauze pads.

You wash the wounds with a fragrant soap from a pump dispenser and blot them dry. You put a gauze pad over one wound and secure it with the band-aids, but the bigger wound requires two pads and is too wide for the band-aids to hold. You cut one of the dish towels in strips with a kitchen knife and tie them over the gauze.

Feeling exhausted, you sit down on the floor and drift to sleep.

You're not sure how long you napped, but the sun is setting Your mouth is dry and tastes like you'd been gnawing on dead bodies. You lean to the side peek out through what's left of the patio door, and to your dismay, you see dogs pacing as if on guard.

You sit and stare at the wall for a long while. A thump against the barrier at the patio door snaps you from your fugue. Your vision clears and you see a row of hooks on the wall near the garage door. You sit up, eyes wide. Car keys.

A rush of excitement invigorates you as a quick plan forms. You get up and hobble over to the keys. Your wounds are throbbing and your muscles have stiffened, making movement difficult and painful. There are three key rings. You saw only one car was in the garage, though, so the first thing to do is find the right set.

Each set has a fob. You take all three, open the door and press the unlock buttons. The first and third fobs are good. You set the other one on the counter and glance up. There is a garage door opener attached to the ceiling. With no electricity, you'll need to open the door manually.

As fast as your wounded body allows, you step into the garage and make your way behind the car. You step up on the bumper and climb up on the trunk. You reach for the manual release for the overhead door, then grab the metal ribs and haul it up one panel at a time.

To your surprise, a pack of smaller dogs is pacing the driveway. They watch you, anticipating your next move. Glancing at the car door, you make your decision, press the unlock tab on the fob, just in case and jump down.

The dogs react in an instant, but you've got a lead. You rip the door open and jump in, smacking the side of your head in your haste. You pull the door shut as a beagle leaps at you. You pin its body between the door and the frame, inches before its teeth would've snapped closed on your arm.

Unwilling to take a chance on reopening the door, you hold it tight as you slide the key into the ignition. Amidst the barking and howling of your pursuers, the engine starts and you yank the stick into reverse.

The beagle squirms to get at you, but you pull tighter and direct your attention to the rearview mirror. The car rolls back. You hear a *thud* as some of the dogs leap at the car. You reach the street, shift into drive and give it gas. The car lurches forward.

The pack gives chase. As the distance increases, you remember the beagle. Turning in your seat, you lift your left leg near the dog and open the door. You kick the dog out, slam the door shut and head for home.

Once in your driveway, you breathe easier, until you hear a distant howl. It spurs you into action. You leap from the car and race for the front door. You fumble with your keys, chastising yourself for not having them in your hand already.

The hairs on the back of your neck stand up as your shaking hand attempts to insert the key. When you finally slide it home, you twist it and push on the door, but it doesn't give. You scream in frustration as you remember the deadbolt. Afraid to look behind you, you begin to pant like your pursuers as you unlock the deadbolt, push the door open and slam it behind you.

You slump to the floor, physically and mentally exhausted. You realize you're going to need a new philosophy for dealing with this new world and as soon as you stop shaking, you're going to sit down and make a list of items you need to face the potential threats your now-overworked imagination envisions.

Go to Chapter 2 page 108

1B1a1b2) You make a split-second decision to seek safety inside the house. You leap onto the deck and go for the patio door, but you didn't think about how you'd get in.

Your first thought is to try the door. Of course, it's locked. You glance back and your anxiety increases as you see a German Shepherd climbing the fence, spurring you to move faster. You search for something to smash the window with.

The usual items are on the deck. A patio table and chairs with a center umbrella, two lounge chairs, and an expensive grill. What to grab? With the German shepherd now over the fence, you grab a chair.

It is bottom-heavy and awkward to wield, making it difficult to generate the speed and force necessary to break the glass. The glass door stays intact and the chair bounces back, almost knocking you down.

The shepherd bounds toward you, reaching the deck. You pick the chair up and swing it backward, making solid contact with the dog. It is sent off the patio and onto the grass, giving you a few precious seconds to try again to break the glass. You wind up to fling the chair at the door when you notice the Jack Russell emerging from under the fence and racing toward you. Time is running out. If it doesn't work this time, you'll have two dogs to deal with.

You release the chair, but the angle is all wrong. It hits and ricochets to the opposite side of the deck.

"Shit!"

Both the shepherd and the terrier are on the steps of the deck. You race for the far end and vault over the railing. You land awkwardly but manage to keep your feet moving. Before you can right yourself, your foot catches a rock. You fall face first but manage to tuck your shoulder and roll. You land on your butt, facing the deck.

The two dogs chase you on the deck but are too late. They turn, heading back toward the steps to the deck. Once again, you have seconds to react.

As you rise, your hand hits the stone you tripped over. In front of you is a door you assume leads to the garage. You see a window in the top, and in a flash, the idea strikes. You snatch up the stone as you stand, draw your arm back to hurl it at the window, but stop. Something feels wrong about the stone. It's too lightweight, but then, you understand why.

You race for the door while your fingers search for the secret compartment.

"Come on," you say, fumbling for a seam. Then, with the dogs not twenty feet away, the panel slides back, revealing a key. *Now, if only it works on this door,* you think. You jam the key into the lock, and God be praised, the knob turns. You breathe a sigh of relief; however, before you can open the door, the dogs reach you and launch a joint assault.

You kick back and deflect the shepherd, but the Jack Russell leaps at you, its jaws snapping at your face. You pull back and the beast slams into you, knocking you against the door. You swat the dog to the side and turn your attention to the shepherd.

As the dog charges, you swing the door open, step inside, and slam it shut behind you. Though you managed to keep the terrier out, the shepherd made it in. You throw the worthless stone at it, then run for the parked car. You pray the door is open. *Who locks the car door once they're in the garage?* You reach the driver's door just as the shepherd races around the front.

You yank the door open as the dog leaps for you. The shepherd hits hard enough to smash the door against your leg. You shout in pain, more from the expected than the actual, and dive inside. As you reach for the door, the shepherd lunges and bites your arm. You cry out and yank your arm back, knowing if you can't close the door, the dog will tear you apart.

Reaching across with your right arm, you try again, but pull back just as the next attack occurs. The teeth snap shut, barely missing your arm. With one last try, you catch the handle. Pulling it closed, the door catches the shepherd and pins it against the frame. The shepherd yelps, then whimpers. As you push the door open to smash the dog again, it backs away.

You close it hard and lock it for good measure before slumping in the seat, exhausted. Sweat pours down your face as if you're standing under a shower. You gasp, feeling the sting as it trickles into some of the bites.

The combination of your heavy breathing and your body heat fogs the windows. You move your arm and wince with the pain. The bite is bleeding. You look for something in the car to use as a bandage. Tearing off the sleeves of a flannel shirt laying on the back seat, you blot the wound, then tie it off as best as you can. Done, you recline the seat far enough for you to lie down.

At some point, you'll have to find antibacterial ointment for the wound. With no medical treatment available, infections are deadly. You'll also have to face the shepherd pacing the garage like a caged lion. But not now. Now is the time for rest and planning. Even the simplest tasks are more difficult than before the apocalypse.

You close your eyes and soon fall into deep and troubled sleep.

You wake a short while later, feeling feverish. You know instantly at least one of the wounds is infected. You need to clean and disinfect them as soon as possible. The longer you wait, the worse it will get.

You sit up and see the shepherd lying down in front of the back door. You eye the side door into the house. You think you can make it and you hope it's unlocked. If not, you don't know if you have the energy for another fight with a dog.

You check under the visors, in the glove box and the center console for car keys, but don't find any. You think about hotwiring the ignition, but you don't have any idea how.

Eyeing the door again, you have an idea. The passenger side door will almost reach the wall when it's open. There is a metal shelving unit next to the door. If you can get out fast enough and pull it away from the wall, you can keep the dog from getting to you.

Though you don't feel much like moving, you know you need to do something for that very reason. You will only get more lethargic as time passes. The blood loss will have a cumulative effect.

You lift your aching legs over the console and scoot into the passenger seat. You put a hand on the door handle and check the dog. Its head is up, eyes locked on you.

You steel your resolve, throw open the door, and jump out. The dog is up in an instant, barking and charging at you. You notice that although the door almost reaches the wall, there is a large open gap underneath. Do you:

1B1a1a2a) go for the door? Page 94

1B1a1a2b) pull out the shelving unit? Page 99

1B1a1b3) You do a quick scan of the yard. House, shed, fence, deck…what is the best choice? A German shepherd scales the fence. Others are trying to dig a hole under it. You don't have much time.

You have no safe place to make a stand and no weapon. Since the dogs are on the far side of the house, you decide to try to run home before they catch you.

You race for the opposite fence and scale it in seconds. Once on the ground, you break right. Your legs stretch for long strides; your arms pump ferociously. You reach the corner and make another right, glancing down the street to see the pack of dogs again pursuing you.

You lose sight of them as you pass in front of the first house. You have an idea. You angle toward the driveway of the second house, disappearing before the dogs are in view. You hop the fence and race to the left and climb the side fence into the next yard.

You hear dogs barking, but still don't see them. Hopping the side fences in every yard, you eventually come to the next street. You must cross the street to get home, but that will leave you in the open. You crouch and peer through the fencing. You still don't see them, which is a relief, but you're worried because you no longer hear them at all. Are they still there? Did they move on? Are *they* listening for *you*?

Fear keeps you frozen for long, nerve-racking minutes, but you have to move. To stay means to risk discovery and or to be trapped. You don't want to be on the street after dark. You'd never hear them coming.

With reluctance, you climb the fence and find the ground below your feet. You opt for slow and quiet instead of fast and noisy. You creep away from the fence, knowing with each step, your safety is threatened. You reach the strip of grass between the sidewalk and the street. You have entered no man's land.

As you edge closer to the street, you hear the chorus of low feral growls. Not wanting to look but needing to, you glance over your shoulder to see the entire pack standing on the lawn of the corner house.

Your bladder threatens to release. Your legs turn to rubber. You look at the house across the street and estimate your chances of making it. You have another split-second decision to make. Do you:

1B1a1a3a) go back? Page 30

1B1a1a3b) try to make it? Page 34

1B1a1a3a) You turn and run for the fence, the dogs gaining. The race will be a tight one. Already you're regretting your choice, but it's too late now. You will your legs to go faster. You leap for the fence as the golden retriever lunges at you. Your leg strikes the golden and you fall short, landing inches from the fence. Your leg skids under the fence, jeans snagging on the bottom links.

You pivot to face your attackers, knowing death by dog pack will be horrendous. By a stroke of luck, your pants tear free. You kick a mixed breed dog and swing your leg up to the crossbar. The golden has recovered, though, and closes its teeth around your ankle.

You cry out in pain as the dog yanks you down. You know if you give up your perch at the top of the fence, you will die. You lift your leg, but the dog still holds tight, whipping its head back and forth like it's playing with a toy. You snap your leg down and back up. The golden still has your pant leg, but you fall to the other side of the fence, dragging the dog with you. It is now hanging by its teeth, but its grip is awkward. Your position isn't any better; you are on your back with your leg in the air.

Dog muzzles press all along the metal fence, snarling and snapping at you. With your free leg, you kick the fence and the dogs back away for an instant before coming back even more riled. The golden's hind legs are pumping, searching for purchase. Its body thuds against the fence. As it makes contact, its paws grab between the rectangular links. You kick at the dog's paws, and this time, the dog arches away and releases its teeth from your pants. You roll free as the barking intensifies.

Backing up, you come to a two-tier decorative wall around a landscaped plot. You reach for a rectangular stone and find it glued in place. *Nothing is ever easy!* You try again and unearth two attached stones. *Good enough.* Taking two running steps to build up momentum, you hurl the stones at the patio door and the glass explodes.

Stepping with care through the jagged opening, you do a quick scan. You need something to put in front of the hole. There is no kitchen table, so you pull the refrigerator out from the wall and reach back to unplug it.

It's on wheels, and you can easily move it across the tiled floor.

You get it to the window just as the German shepherd leaps through. Startled, you pause for an instant, but you know you need to close the hole before more dogs make it inside. Better to deal with one dog than an entire pack.

The shepherd's claws scrabble on the hard, smooth surface, giving you time to slam the refrigerator in place. You position it just as the shepherd launches at you. It is airborne and you sidestep and swat it on the side of the head, knocking it to the ground. You look for an avenue of escape but end up in the middle of the kitchen behind the island. Your first thought is to climb on top of it, out of reach of the vicious dog. Then you see the hanging rack of pots and pans suspended from the ceiling.

You yank one down and face your four-legged opponent. It backs you into a corner and lunges at you. You swing the pan like a baseball bat and connect a solid hit. The shepherd flips and lands, stunned. You advance, not giving it a chance to regain its bearings. You open the door to the garage, shove the dog over the threshold with the pan and close the door.

While the other dogs howl outside, you sit down on a bar chair at the island and put your head on your arms. What a nightmare. *What the hell do you do now?*

Unable to form thoughts for a long while, you sit and stare at the wall. A thump against the barrier at the patio door snaps you from your fugue. Your vision clears and you focus on a row of hooks attached to the wall near the garage door. You sit up as recognition arrives. Car keys.

A rush of excitement invigorates you as quick plan forms, but it all depends on where the dog is. You get up and hobble to the keys. The wounds and your muscles have stiffened, making movement difficult and painful. You find three sets of keys, but there's only one car in the garage. Each set as a fob. You open the door a crack and press the unlock buttons on each one. The first and third set work for the car. You set the other set on the counter and glance up. There is a garage door opener attached to the ceiling. With no electricity, the door will have to be opened manually. That means you'll have to face the shepherd again.

As if reading your mind, the shepherd growls. You close the door.

Your eyes light on a frying pan. You stand behind the door and pull it toward you, hoping the dog will run in and you can duck out and lock it inside, but of course, that doesn't happen. You peek into the garage, and although you hear growling, you don't see the dog.

As fast as your wounded body allows, you step into the garage and make your way to the rear of the car. You hear scrabbling on the cement floor. The shepherd is in motion. You step up the bumper and climb on the trunk just as the dog arrives. It tries to jump up, snapping at your heels, but finds no purchase. You swing the pan and it ducks out of the way.

Standing on the trunk, you reach the overhead door release. Hand over hand, grabbing the metal panels, you lift the door. With daylight pouring in, the shepherd runs out. It stops and faces you, barking ferociously.

You jump down, and the dog sprints at you. Panic rises once more. You fling the pan at it and jump in the passenger seat, shutting the door before the dog gets to you. It stands on hind legs against the passenger window, barking non-stop.

You settle into the driver's seat, insert the key and are about to start it when a large dog jumps up on the driver's side window. Your heart skipping a beat, you scream in shock. You twist the key, saying a silent prayer and the engine turns over.

Without a hesitation, you slip the stick into reverse and floor it. The car bounces over a doggy speed bump. You are down the driveway in seconds. The dogs follow. You shift into drive, flip the dogs off and head for home. For a while, you see a small pack chasing the car, and for a moment you fear they will follow you all the way home, but the numbers dwindle and soon only the shepherd is left.

A few quick turns and added speed and you lose the dog...you hope. You park in front of the house, find your keys in a pocket, and look around. Still no dogs. You get out and limp as fast as you can to the house. You lock the doors and go about taking care of your injuries. You wonder if it will ever be safe to leave the house again.

It is then you determine that to survive, you need a much better plan than just wandering around. With your wounds cleansed and bandaged, you sit down and prop your leg up on a pillow and begin making a list of things you need. (See list on page 209)

Go to Chapter 2 Page 108

1B1a1a3b) You take a tentative step into the street, keeping your gaze fixed on the dogs. They have not yet moved and are eyeing you like an entree. A second step and still no movement. Your third step, however, causes the entire pack to inch toward you. They match your next move as well.

You swallow hard, knowing you have little chance of retreat. It is move forward or die. You eye the ground in front of you and estimate the number of necessary steps. At a run, you'll need five steps to clear the street; twenty-five long strides to cross the front yard and reach the fence. How many will it take the pack to close the distance and take you down? You have little choice but to try to make it.

You steel yourself for the sprint, and after sucking in a deep breath, you go for it. In two stride lengths, you are at a full sprint. You are too afraid to look back. Besides, it will slow you down. Don't worry…you'll know when they are close. They'll be snapping at your heels.

You race across the yard, counting each stride, but quickly lose track. A high-pitched hysterical scream that you don't recognize as your own erupts from your core. The fence is close now, maybe only five more strides away. Then it happens. Something connects with your legs and you go down in a rolling heap. When you finally come to a stop, your back is to the fence. You kick and flail wildly as the animals close around you. There are so many of them and you make contact with every swing and kick.

Teeth clamp down. You keep moving to be a harder target. Staying where you are is not an option. Again, from somewhere deep inside you, another sound explodes, but this time, it is an inhuman feral growl. The animals pause for a moment, just long enough for you to grab the fence and hoist your bloody body to your feet. You plant two hard kicks into some smaller dogs and it gives you enough room to jump up on the fence, but not before getting another deep, ripping bite to your calf.

You fall more than jump down to the grass in the backyard. Unable to move, you lie there, listening to the snarling. After several long minutes, you force yourself sit and then stand. Your entire body

34

is on fire. Blood seeps from the many bites and scrapes.

With waning strength, you hobble to the next fence and climb over. As you cross the yard, you glance back to see the pack still behind you, barking protests at your escape.

Fence after fence, you draw closer to home. You stop at the fence in the last yard. You can see your house across the street and three houses down to the right. You place your foot on the lower crossbar and look behind you. Most of the dogs are still there. If more should come around the corner now, you wouldn't have the strength to fend them off. You would go down and die.

Is it worth the risk? It is getting harder to think. You've lost a lot of blood. Do you:

1B1a1a3b1) stay and rest? Page 36

1B1a1a3b2) risk going home? Page 39

1B1a1a3b1) You don't have the strength to climb or the nerve to risk the final jaunt. You move to the house and sit in a patio chair. Just a little rest; that's all you need, you tell yourself. Your eyes grow heavy. You snap them open, but the time between drifting off and waking becomes shorter. Soon your eyes close and you cannot fight the sweet pull of sleep.

You dream of your family—your spouse, your son. They appear before your eyes. So real. You are happy. The pain of your wounds drifts away, replaced by a strange euphoria. You reach out for your spouse's extended hand and feel it in your own. You are surprised by the sensation, but don't question it. Your son runs to you, throwing his arms around your neck. He laughs and holds you tight. Tears run down your face. Your spouse wipes them away and kisses you.

A brilliant light blooms behind them and the three of you turn and walk toward it. You have never felt better in your life.

A loud and alien sound enters your dream. You look behind you to see something dark crouching in the shadows. Your spouse places a hand on your face and turns your focus toward the light. You hear it again; a louder, fiercer distant memory surges.

You stop and turn.

From somewhere in your mind, your spouse's voice shouts, "No!" as your eyes fly open. It takes a moment for you to awaken and become alert, and when you do, you see a line of dogs glaring at you through the fence.

You jolt to a standing position, but the effort leaves you dizzy. You feel weak and can barely stand. Your movement throws the dogs into a frenzy. They bark, snarl, and snap. A few of them try to climb the fence.

You back up to the patio door, and to your relief, find it unlocked. You step inside, close and lock the door behind you, then pull the blinds. You lean on the kitchen island for balance. Looking down, you see a small pool of blood forming on the floor. *How much blood have I lost?* You need to stop the flow or you will bleed out. It may already be too late.

You stumble forward, forcing your legs to hold your weight, and search the cupboards. Empty. You grab a bottle of hand sanitizer from the countertop. Opening the fridge, you find a half empty jug of orange juice. You take that, too, sniffing it as you walk toward the stairs. It doesn't smell bad. The date on the carton has not yet expired, but the electricity has been off for two days. How long would it be before the juice spoiled?

You risk a sip. It tastes fine. You take bigger gulps, juice sloshing down your face to the carpeted steps. You force yourself to stop drinking so you can save some in case you find some meds and need to swallow them down.

You barely make it to the bathroom at the top of the stairs. You search the cabinets but find no medical supplies. The next two rooms are bedrooms. Again, you come up empty. The farthest door leads to the master bedroom. In the attached bathroom, you find a full box of bandages, including three butterfly strips and gauze pads, and a tube of triple antibiotic cream.

Stripping your clothes off, you examine your wounds, identifying the worst ones. You find a clean washcloth, place it under the faucet and turn the spigot. You don't expect much of a flow, but even a little bit will help. Enough water runs out to dampen the cloth, and then you shut it off.

Gently you clean the cuts and bites. The largest one is too wide to close with the butterfly strips, so you press a gauze pad to it. It comes away soaked. You coat the wound with the antibiotic cream, place two clean pads over it, and wind a roll of gauze around it as tight as you can. After you tend to all the wounds, you rummage through the medicine cabinet and the drawers under the sink. You find aspirin, pain pills, and a plastic prescription bottle labeled Amoxicillin. You can remember taking that antibiotic a time or two, but not the reason why it was prescribed for you. Still, in your expert medical opinion, it's better to take something rather than nothing. You swallow one with the orange juice and debate doubling the dosage but decide against it. You take two aspirin with the remaining juice, then go back to the bedroom.

You stare at the bed for a moment, not sure if you should surrender to sleep for fear of never waking. You debate the pros and cons with yourself for several minutes, but in the end, you choose sleep. You need rest to heal.

You crawl into bed, get comfortable, and notice some blood seepage on the gauze pads over the big wound. Sticking a pillow under your leg, you close your eyes. Within seconds, you are asleep. Images of your spouse and son play before you again. You reach out for their extended hands, but you can't quite touch them.

Go to Chapter 2 page 108

1B1a1a3b2) Looking outside two minutes later, the street still looks safe. With as much stealth as you can muster from your exhausted and bleeding body, you slide to the sidewalk. Your foot touches but you knee buckles, and you grip the top fence post to prevent a fall.

With a glance in both directions, you leave the safety of the yard and make a break for it. You reach the street and head toward your house. You get to the middle of the street when you hear the growl. You want to look back, but force your eyes to remain forward.

Increasing your speed, you reach the opposite curb. You are now only two houses away from yours now. Your mind speeds through your options. You have the key to the front door, but it might take some time to get it open. You are relatively sure the side door leading into the garage is open. You know the patio door is unlocked, but you'll have to get through the gate. No matter what you decide to do, it will take time.

Now you risk a glance back. The pack is coming, and fast.

Your force your aching body into a run. You'll be able to reach the front door for sure before they arrive. You might be able to reach the side door, but it will be close. There's not much chance of reaching the gate. Do you:

1B1a1a3b2a) for the front door? Page 40

1B1a1a3b2b) take a chance on the side door? Page 42

1B1a1a3b2c) risk going to the gate? Page 43

1B1a1a3b2a) You reach into your pocket to retrieve your keys. You wish the front door had a fob function that you could just click open. You have the key in a death grip to prevent accidentally dropping it. You are ten steps from the porch with the dogs right behind you.

Ahead, your eyes fall on the Happy Easter sign with the rabbit atop the four-foot high decorative metal pole. You remember buying it two years ago for your spouse, but more importantly, you remember the sharp points at the bottom of the pole.

You grab and yank it from the ground as you leap for the porch. As soon as your feet touch down, you whirl and thrust the two sharpened prongs like a spear in front of you. You hold it in one hand and balance it on the wrist of the other. The shepherd leaps and you jab the pole at it as hard as you can through its neck.

The dog yelps and whines, suspended from the spear. Its weight makes the pole difficult to wield and the point dips. You sweep it across the pack, knocking several dogs off the porch. A small mixed breed gets around the pole, but you kick it, sending it flying.

With the pack at bay for the moment, you reach behind with one hand and try to insert the key. You miss and try again with the same result. You realize it's an impossible task with your attention elsewhere and the pole heavy and hard to balance with one hand, so you lift the spear and toss it, dog and all, into the middle of the pack. Turning, you line up the key, drive it home and twist the knob. The door does not budge, and you curse yourself for forgetting about the deadbolt. Without looking, you kick backward, striking another dog.

You fumble to put the key in the second lock. It slides in and you twist it. You turn the door knob again. This time it opens, but before you can enter, a dog latches onto your leg. You kick it free and stagger through the door, slamming it shut. You catch one of its legs. It cracks audibly as the dog howls and falls away, allowing you to close the door.

You engage both locks and lean against the door, panting. Outside the door, you hear vicious snarls and growls. A dog yelps and you realize what's happening. The other dogs are tearing the wounded ones apart. Survival of the fittest in practice.

There is a puddle of congealing blood on the wood floor. You hobble into the kitchen and take four bottles of water from the warm refrigerator, then climb upstairs. In the master bath, you find what you need and sit on the edge of the tub to clean and bandage the wounds. The worst one is too wide to close, so you rely on compression. After dousing it with peroxide, you apply a liberal amount of antibiotic cream. You tie gauze around the pads and pull tight. It's the best you can do.

After downing several pain pills and a bottle of water, you walk to the bed, put a towel down under a pillow and prop up your wounded leg. You fall asleep, praying you will wake up in the morning.

Go to Chapter 2 Page 108

1B1a1a3b2b) You angle across the front lawn toward the far side of the house. You're sure the side door is unlocked. You won't need the key. If you can reach it in time, it will be easy to get inside to safety. You turn the corner and hear the dogs close behind. The side door is only a few steps away. You grab the door knob, turn and push. Your head recoils after bouncing off the door. It won't budge, no matter how hard you ram it. You fumble for your keys as the first dog attacks.

You scream as its teeth rip into your flesh. You punch at it, but another one leaps on you. You toss it aside, desperately digging in your pocket for the keys. You pull your hand out, but before you can insert the right one, another dog latches onto your arm and the keys fall.

"No!" You shout and reach for them, but two more dogs join in the frenzy. Your fingertips graze the keys on the ground, but your arm is pulled away. Pain is everywhere. You are unable to stop your howling. Your leg gives way and you drop to one knee. The keys are right in front of you, but just out of reach. As more dogs arrive for the feast, you are driven to the ground. You continue to struggle and kick, but your strength wanes and you are rendered defenseless.

Your final thought is the memory of locking the garage door when you took out the garbage four days ago. You wonder why you would have done that as your vision narrows and everything grows darker. You never lock that door. The lights dim, fade and extinguish.

End

1B1a1a3b2c) You race across your lawn and around the corner of the house. The dogs are close. The gate is right in front of you. You're almost there. You make a mental list of what you need to do. Lift latch. Push gate. Pivot. Slam gate shut. Lower latch. *You've got this.* Then, the first dog rams you from behind. You trip and fall, rolling with the shepherd.

You push it aside and get to your feet, but three more dogs come at you and knock you back down. You struggle, punch and kick, but the dogs are everywhere. You can't get two consecutive seconds to rise and escape.

Fighting with all your remaining strength; your fear and desperation fueling a last-chance effort, you manage to get to your knees. You grab one dog around the neck before its teeth snap shut on your face and pitch it against the house. Stunned, it slides to the ground. Again, you try to rise, but there's that damn German shepherd again. As you push yourself up, the shepherd launches at you, closing its teeth around your neck. You have a sudden urge to vomit and might have, had not the shepherd ripped out your throat.

End

1B1a1b) You run for the side of the house and toward the backyard. There is a split rail fence with other fencing attached. To your dismay, you notice the fence barely reaches the ground. The dogs will be able to dig underneath with ease.

You reach the fence as the dogs close in. You place your hands on the top rail and swing your legs up and over like a gymnast. You land and run. For the moment, you're safe. You see a shed to your right. You have three options. Do you:

1B1a1b1) go to the shed? Page 19
1B1a1b2) try to get in the house? Page 24
1B1a1b3) hop the far side fence and make another run for it? Page 28

1B1a2) You see a parked car on the street to your left. It is the closest possibility that might offer safety, but it could be locked. Still, you veer toward it at full speed. You have a lead on the dogs, and you have a few seconds to check the car, but not enough time if you make a mistake. You reach the car, a Honda Civic, and try the door. It's locked. You swear. You see an SUV of some sort two houses down, and make a run for it.

You reach the SUV with seconds to spare. Tugging on the door, you find it doesn't open. Do you:

1B1a2a) run to the next vehicle you see? Page 46

1B1a2b) climb the roof? Page 47

1B1a2a) With the dogs close on your heels, you sprint toward the next and last vehicle you see, a minivan. You race for all your worth, but soon there are paws pouncing next to you. It's a German shepherd and it gives you a look as if to say, "Where do you think you're going?"

The shepherd angles toward you. You reach down and swat at it, knocking yourself off balance in the process. Another dog bolts in front of you. Trying to avoid it, you trip and fall hard on the street. You roll several times, picking up a multitude of bruises. The asphalt tears long ruts of skin from your arms and hands. You scrape your face on the loose gravel and debris. By the time you stop sliding, the abrasions and bites all over your body are throbbing and burning.

You roll to your back and kick one dog as another one rips into your arm. You flail wildly and manage to keep them at bay momentarily, but as soon as you try to rise, they dart in and take you down again. The pain is severe. You heave yourself onto hands and knees to crawl away, but there are too many of them and soon, you are overcome by their weight and the viciousness of the attack. One by one, they dart in, bite and rend, and back away as another moves in.

How did these animals become feral in such a short time? you wonder as your consciousness slips away. You make one last desperate effort to get to your feet and run, but one of the dogs buries its teeth into your wrist. As you punch at it, the dog opens your vein. Blood is everywhere. You know time is short. You manage to get to your feet, but you cannot defend yourself any longer. With one hand pressed over the spurting wound, you try to run, but no longer have the strength. After only a few steps, you stagger, from either the overwhelming exhaustion or from the dog attack.

In the end, it doesn't matter. Soon, you are no longer aware of the pain or the sound of your ripping flesh. You close your eyes and welcome death.

End

1B1a2b) You race around the SUV and put your foot on the rear bumper. You grab the luggage rack with both hands and pull yourself upward, your feet climbing until you are safely on top. You lie there panting, never so scared in your life. Then you hear the claws scrabbling on the metal.

You lift your head to see many of the dogs standing on their hind paws with their front ones on the SUV. Some are jumping against the truck. and the smaller ones don't stand a chance of making it up on the hood, but several, like the shepherd and the golden retriever, are tall enough to make it if they get any footing. You know the Jack Russell can jump higher than all of them.

You watch their progress while you catch your breath. You look around, analyzing the situation. How long will it take before the dogs lose interest and go off to find a more accessible source of food? A few of the dogs sit and watch, their tongues hanging out, panting. Several lie down, but all eyes are on you.

You notice foam on some of their mouths. Is it just from the effort of running, or are they being driven mad by infection? Is that how the dogs were affected by the disease that killed off the humans? What about other animals? You'll have to consider that, providing you survive this encounter.

The SUV has a sunroof, and it gives you an idea. You crawl forward and peer inside. You gasp, seeing a woman's body in the driver's seat. *Is she alive?* You knock on the sunroof, but get no response. You watch to see if her chest rises and falls, but there is no movement. However, there is a key. A new hope awakens within you. If you can get inside the SUV, you can drive away. The question is, how do you do that? You pound the glass with your fist, raising a new round of barking from the gathered diners. They renew their efforts to get at you, as if understanding your plan.

The glass is too thick to break with your hand, so you stand and try to stomp through it. Over and over, you drive the heel of your shoe into the center of the glass to no avail. Exhausted, you sit down to think of a new plan.

The dogs quiet down and watch you, waiting. You dig out your keys and try to figure out how best to hold them to deliver a forceful blow to the glass without cutting your fingers. You make a few soft strikes. The solid sound of contact gives you confidence. You raise your arm higher and bring it down with a resounding crack, jamming a key back against your fingers and carving a deep gash into the middle one. You cry out and release the keys, which go flying. In desperate effort to regain them, you reach out over the side and almost lose your balance. You grab them, just inches from the Jack Russell, who leaps high enough to have bitten a chunk out of your nose, had you not jerked away in time.

The other dogs gather below you, all up on hind legs, barking and leaping as they anticipate fresh meat. The shepherd shoves its way in, as does the golden. With no leverage and having to rely on abdominal muscles that have long ago gone soft, it takes a great effort to pull yourself back to safety, but not before the shepherd lunges an inch from your face. You feel its foul, hot breath on your neck and hear the audible snap of sharp teeth at your neck. You roll on your back and stare at the sky. Your body shakes with surging adrenaline and fear as you understand how close to death you were.

It is a long time before you can move again. The dogs are dancing around the car, certain you'll make another mistake. You get to your knees, afraid to stand for fear of losing your balance. Positioning the key in your fist, thumb on top, you drive it repeatedly into the glass. After a good twenty strikes, the first spider web appears. The sight reinvigorates you. Soon, the cracks weave across the length of the sunroof. When the key finally punches through, you shout with joy.

"Yes!"

You swipe the key around the edge of the tiny hole to widen it, but it takes too long. You stand and make a few cautious stomps. Then, impatient, you raise your foot and slam it down, breaking the glass and jamming your leg through. Taken by surprise, you fall on your butt and begin to slide over the edge, however, you are stuck and you feel the shards of glass biting into your leg in several places. Your upper body is hanging over the side, pulling your leg and causing the glass to dig deeper into your skin. You let go of the keys because you need both hands to push on the roof. You manage to get back on top and sit up, but now you're stuck. Do you:

1B1a2b1) yank your leg out? Page 50

1B1a2b2) work the key around the opening? Page 51

1B1a2b3) lie back and cry? Page 53

1B1a2b1) Well, that was dumb. What did you think was going to happen? You sever an artery and bleed out in minutes. You should have known better. This was an easy one.

Game over.

1B1a2b2) You look where you feel the glass poking you. You push your leg farther into the sunroof to lessen the pain and pressure, pick the key ring up, then press the longest key against each point of contact. It is painstaking and painful. You feel the warm blood trickle down your leg inside your pants and pray none of the cuts are too severe.

Fifteen minutes later, you slowly pull your leg free. Blood has soaked the back of your pants. You stand, unfasten and drop them to your ankles. Streaks of blood are drying on your leg. You find small punctures up and down your thigh, but there is one on your calf that you must have gotten when you broke through. Most of the wounds are not serious, but a few are still seeping.

You blow out a sigh of relief and thank God you hadn't gone with your first thought of yanking the leg free. (Yep; that was a slam to those who chose the first option.) That would've been dumb. The smell from the woman's decaying body rises, making you flinch back and gag, which is a shock. She didn't look like she was that ripe when you first saw her. You press the pants to the wounds on your leg with one hand and hold your breath while trying to clear away the remaining shards of glass. The task is made more difficult by having to suck in and hold a new breath every few minutes.

The dogs are watching silently now. Many have resumed sitting or lying down to save energy. The glass cleared away, you slip both legs through the opening and lower yourself through the opening.

"Better luck next time, mutts."

They ignore you.

Once inside and surprisingly taking no further damage, you wrap the pants around your hand and wipe the glass from the seat.

The next task is to get the body out of the car before you hurl all over the upholstery.

You unfasten her seat belt and turn the key to lower the window. Instantly the dogs jump at the glass. You lift and push her head out, and the dogs go into a frenzy. A few of the bigger dogs and the ones that are high jumpers catch pieces of her, but not enough to help pull her out.

You get your hands under her butt and push, a chore made more difficult by the rigor mortis. Once the body is halfway out the window, the dogs do the rest. You raise the window, clear off the small shards of glass on the seat, and settle into it. You ignore the pain in your legs and start the car, praying the engine will turn over. It does, and you lower your head to the steering wheel, exhaling with relief and offering a prayer of thanks.

Shifting into gear, you stomp the accelerator and speed off, bouncing over a few doggy speed bumps. Glancing in the rearview mirror, you see most of the dogs are busy with the body, but a few stubborn animals give chase. Speeding around the corner, you head for home.

A minute later, you pull into the driveway. After you scan all mirrors to make sure no strays have followed, you open the door. On shaky legs and with an unsteady hand, you manage to fit the key into the two locks and open the door. You step into safety, lock the door behind you, and slide to the floor where the adrenaline drains and the events of the day take their toll. You break down in tears. Now it's okay to cry.

Go to Chapter 2 Page 95

1B1a2b3) You're done? You big baby. *Seriously?* I know you're frustrated, but there's no crying in the apocalypse. Do or do not; there is no cry. Now go back and choose one of the other two options.

1B1c) & 1B1a3) Outrun the dogs? Get real! You didn't think this through. Fear takes over, and in your panic, you turn and run. Reaching the corner, you cut across the lawn and head for the next street. Too late, you realize this was a bad idea. *Why didn't I go for the cars?*

You angle toward the fenced yard. It is your only chance to survive. You reach the fence and are about to hop it, when something solid bowls you over. You tumble to the ground and try to rise. The rest of the pack arrives and they drag you down. You fight with a ferocity you didn't know you possessed, biting one dog on the leg before it can remove your nose. No matter how hard you fight, you can't break free. The bites multiply and the pain intensifies. Then, the German shepherd appears out of nowhere and your scream abruptly ends as it tears your throat out.

End

1B1b) You back away, your palms up and out to the sides in what you hope is a nonthreatening posture. The dogs watch you and slowly approach. You continue to move backward, but a little faster. They speed up when you do, stalking you like the prey you are.

This is getting you nowhere fast. It's obvious they are going to pursue. Before the impending attack begins, you want to get as far away as possible. Figuring on a one-second head start, you turn and run. Do you:

1B1b1) veer toward a house? Page 18

1B1b2) head for a parked car? Page 56

1B1b2) You glance around at the houses and decide the closest source of safety is one of the parked cars. You sprint toward the first one, but seeing a body in the driver's seat, you choose to bypass that one. The next vehicle is two car lengths back. You estimate you have enough time to make it, but it's not a guess you want to be wrong about.

You reach the door and it dawns on you this might have been a mistake. What if the door is locked? The door opens and a sob of relief escapes you. You jump in and close the door just as the pack arrives. You close your eyes as the dogs bark and growl. Their claws scrape on the metal and you envision them leaping at the body to get at you.

Then, a new sound startles you alert. You see a German shepherd has climbed halfway in the wide-open passenger window. You shrink back, pressing against the door. To your horror, the shepherd gains traction and its front paws reach the seat.

You lift your feet and begin pummeling the beast's head in rapid succession, as if pumping the pedals of a bike at full speed. Your constant scream fills the car. You land blows to the dog as it attempts to bite. You aren't doing much damage, but at least you've stopped the shepherd's progress.

Changing your target, you aim for its legs, keeping the dog jumping. Its balance changes, teetering. You grab the steering wheel for more leverage and your hand brushes something. You risk a glance and see the keys hanging from the ignition. You whoop with delight and reach to turn the ignition when the shepherd clamps down on your shoe.

You wince in expectation, but no pain comes. The dog has the sole across the width. It gives your foot a violent shake and snarls. You turn the key and the engine roars to life. Reaching behind without looking, you trigger the automatic window. The glass behind your head moves. Wrong window. You move your hand and try again. This time the passenger window moans and struggles to rise under the weight of the animal. You worry it will not have enough power to finish its ascension, but it changes the balance of the dog and it slides out the window.

It makes a valiant effort to keep a grip on your foot, but as it falls from its perch, you are released. The window finishes its rise and you blow out a heavy breath.

Settling into the seat, you shift and feed the gas. You've never been so happy to feel a car move. In the rearview mirror, you see the dogs give chase, but after a few turns they are gone. You pull up in front of your house, check the mirrors, then exit and sprint to the house.

Once inside with the doors locked, you realize you are totally unprepared for this new world. You'd better make some plans before venturing out again.

Go to Chapter 2 page 96

1B2) You want to see if anyone is still alive, so you get in your car and head toward downtown, about two miles away. You see several bodies along your route and you know if something isn't done about them, they will soon draw scavengers in droves and you will have new problems. But first, you must determine if indeed you are the last survivor.

You continue at slow speed in case you see something or someone that requires you to make a quick stop. When you reach the outskirts of town, you hear a gunshot. You brake and search for the location of the shooter. Was it aimed at you? You don't think so, but still you advance with caution. Another shot is fired, this one sounding closer. You are about to turn around when a woman runs out from between two houses. You are elated to find another person. Her arms are full, but you can't tell what she's carrying. Then, a thought strikes you. *If she's not the shooter, then there is at least one other person.*

As soon as this revelation comes to you, a man steps out from where she emerged. He raises his arm and a shot erupts. The woman arches her back and pitches forward. She falls on what she was carrying and crumples on her side. You watch in shock. Then you see her move. She's still alive. Do you:

1B2a) get out and help her? Page 59

1B2b) turn around and drive off? Page 74

1B2c) steer your car the shooter? Page 75

1B2a) The instinct to help a fellow survivor—another human—is overwhelming. You drive closer and get out of the car. The shooter is approaching fast. As you run toward the injured woman, he snaps off a shot that ricochets off the street six feet in front of you.

You pause and second guess your actions as the woman moans and tries to rise. The sight spurs you on. You race toward her. The shooter is closing fast. You reach the woman, grab her under the arms and drag her backward to the car.

To your surprise, the man is less than thirty feet away. He slows and aims his gun at you, but does not fire. Your eyes lock and he lines you up in the sight. You're not sure why he hasn't pulled the trigger, but you don't want to stick around to find out the reason. You reach the car, open the back door behind the driver's seat, and lift and push her inside.

Closing the door, you eye the man who now stands over what the woman dropped. When you went to her, you saw she was carrying bottled water. You hadn't given any thought to it before, but now you realize that food and water supplies are running low, and people would obviously be willing to kill for it.

You shift the vehicle into reverse and see the man shove the gun in his belt and bend to pick up the scattered bottles. There is no doubt in your mind that had you tried to pick up any of the scattered bottles, you'd be dead now. But the reality of the low food and water supply begins to sink in. You need to stock up while you can before there is no more. Food and water will be priceless; those who have it will be the ones in power. Those who have it will also become the prey of those who don't. You need to get back to your house and think things through.

You make it home without further incident and drag the woman from the car. She has left a large bloodstain on the rear seat. Unsure of the extent of her injuries, you get her inside in a hurry. You place her on the kitchen table and roll her over onto her front. The back of her shirt is soaked through with her blood, and you lift it high enough to find the bullet hole just to the right of her spine. You are no doctor, but you know the bullet didn't exit since there is no blood on the front of her shirt. If she is to survive, you must extract the bullet. Even if you do everything right, she still might die. More likely, she'd die faster from your unskilled bulletectomy.

You try to think, but your brain is muddled. Then her eyes open and she chokes out, "Help—me."

You must make a decision, and fast. Do you:

1B2a1) accept there is nothing you can do? Page 61

1B2a2) try to remove the bullet? Page 68

1B2a3) do the humane thing and put her out of her misery? Page 72

1B2a1) You take her hand and whisper, "Everything is going to be all right." You release her hand and run upstairs to retrieve a sleeping pill. You grab a bottle of water from the kitchen, and return to her, lifting her head so she can take the pill. She gets it down, but chokes on the water.

Gently, you place her head back on the floor and go to the family room to get a pillow. When you set it under her head, she cries out in pain. You want to do something, but you're too afraid you'll end up killing her, so you just let her sobbing continue.

You sit with her, offering whatever comfort you can until the sleeping pill kicks in. She drifts off and you go outside to dig another grave on the opposite side of the yard from your spouse and son. By the time you finish, she is dead. You bury her and say a prayer.

Chapter 2

You wake, still shocked at what people do to each other. It did send you a clear message: it's everyone for themselves, and you need a weapon to protect what you have. You find a notebook and sit down on the kitchen floor. You make headings at the top of the first page and begin to list everything you think you will need to survive.

Make your own list and compare it with the one at the end.

With the list done, at least for now, you go down to the basement and begin clearing room for what you'll collect tomorrow. You're aware it is a waste of time, but you want to organize your thoughts, and the dead woman is still on your mind.

Finished, you make breakfast outside on the grill. You fix all six of the eggs, all the remaining bacon, and the last four slices of bread. No sense letting it to go waste. Might as well eat it while it's still good.

The aroma rises and you inhale deeply. Your mouth waters. This will be the best meal you've had in days, if not the best one ever. When the food is ready, you shut down the gas, and realize you forgot to bring out a plate and utensils. You go inside to retrieve them, and when you go back to the patio door, you see a boy of about ten or twelve years old bending over the grill, grabbing your bacon. Do you:

2A) chase the boy away? Page 63

2B) speak to him? Page 66

2A) Anger flashes and a red mist clouds your vision. The sight of someone eating—no, *stealing* your food makes you want to lash out. You step through the doorway, shouting obscenities, and plant a foot on the boy's butt.

"Beat it, you thief," you say and threaten to kick him again.

"But I only want something to eat. I'm starving."

"Then stop whining and go somewhere else. You can't have mine."

The boy cries.

You lift your leg to kick him again and he leaps from the deck, sobbing. He runs four yards down and disappears around the side of a house. You didn't see if he went inside, but you make a mental note to keep a look out for him when you go over there to clean it out.

Congratulations. It only took you how many days to lose your humanity?

You look at your spouse's grave, then at the dead woman's. Their voices ring in your head, "Get him back." You jump from the deck and give chase. He has a head start, but you're sure you can catch him.

Dodging between two houses, you reach the street and stop. You look both ways, but don't see him. Left would bring him back past your house. You doubt he went that way, which leaves only straight and right. On a hunch, you go right.

After passing six houses, you stop. He's either farther ahead than you thought, or he's in one of these houses.

"Hey, kid, I'm sorry. Come on back. I'll fix you some breakfast."

You look around anxiously waiting for a response. You get one, but it's not what you expected.

"Sounds good to me."

You whirl to find a man with a hunting rifle standing on the porch of a house across the street.

"Why don't you lead me to your house? You can fix me breakfast, then give me the rest of the food you have. Doesn't that sound good to you?" He flashes a sinister smile and walks down the steps.

He stops five feet away, holding the rifle loosely but pointed in your general direction. If he's a neighbor, you don't recognize him. He has a sucker in his mouth. His head has recently been shaved. A long dark beard hangs from his chin. He pulls the sucker out and says, "Lead on. I'm hungry."

Your chest constricts, making it difficult to breath. You know if you lead him home, he will have no reason to keep you alive. You turn and walk, your mind flying in hyperdrive, searching for a solution.

The gunshot takes you by surprise. You flinch and wrap your arms around your body, checking for wounds. The second shot shocks you just as much, and you jump like the street was on fire.

The man says, "You stupid bitch."

You turn and see the man is facing away from you. His rifle is at his shoulder and he is sighting on a bloody, naked woman standing on the porch of the house he just left. She is crying and holding the handgun in very shaky hands. She cocks the hammer and aims another shot. They fire simultaneously. The kick throws her backward as if someone yanked on a rope tied around her waist.

The man spins to the side, the rifle flopping. A red spot spreads on his shoulder. You kick him in the back of his knee. It buckles and he falls forward to the pavement.

He tries to raise the rifle, but you are on him. Grabbing and twisting, you tear the rifle from his hands and step back. Cursing, he fumbles at his stomach. He pulls out a gun, and as he swings it in your direction, you lift the rifle and pull the trigger.

The gun kicks, lifting the barrel. The bullet intended for the chest blasts a hole through his eye. He falls back.

You stand frozen in place and stare at the corpse you've created. Then the bile rises and you drop to your knees and vomit. Once the dry heaves have subsided, you walk to the house where the woman's body lies across the threshold, her lifeless eyes up at the ceiling.

This world is too crazy for words. Two more lives lost for no reason. You drag both bodies inside the house and close the door.

At home, you check the rifle's magazine and discover it is empty. You tally the score. Two dead bodies, one lost kid, and one empty magazine. The day's off to a good start.

Maybe you should stick around the house today, get organized and set up some defenses.

Go to Chapter 3 on page 115

2B) "Sit down and eat. I'll get a second plate."

He jumps and pivots. His eyes go wide and dart around for an escape route.

"Relax," you hold up your hands to show you're no threat. "I won't hurt you. If you're hungry, sit down."

You leave him on the deck, but watch him through the kitchen window. He eyes the bacon, but he makes no attempt to snatch any extra. You feel good about your decision.

Outside, you sit across the patio table from him. He is all but a few bites from finishing.

"You must've been starved."

He nods and shovels the last forkful into his mouth. Even before he swallows he is eyeing your plate. You smile, but lean further over your food, just in case.

"Still hungry?"

He nods.

You motion with your head. "Inside there's a bag of apples on the counter. Take a couple."

His eyes swing toward the house, then back to you. He wants the food, but is trying to decide if it's a trick to lure him inside.

"Go. I'm not gonna hurt you. They'll go bad if they aren't eaten soon."

He takes the chance, and seconds later is back, an apple in each hand. He bites into one with a loud crunch. The juice runs down his chin and he wipes it away with a dirty sleeve.

"What's your name?" you ask.

"Andy."

"Andy, I'm Larry (or whatever name you chose). I'm glad to meet someone who's not trying to kill everyone they see. This sure is a crazy world now."

The boy chomps around the apple like it's an ear of corn.

"I take it you haven't eaten in a while. "He shakes his head.

"Which house do you live in?"

He hesitates. His eyes widen and he slows his chewing.

"Hey, I'm not going to rob you or anything. I'm just curious. You're free to leave here and go home whenever you want. I only want to know which one is yours so I don't take your things. I'll skip your house." Having eaten all the apple except for the seeds and the stem, Andy tosses what little core there is far into the yard. He polishes the second apple on his shirt and takes a bite.

"I live four houses down."

You look down the backyards. You know the house but you had never met Andy or his parents.

"You moved in recently, right?"

He nods again.

"Okay, look, I don't know how much you know about what's been going on, but it's really crazy out here. I've only seen one other living person and a few animals, but they are ready to kill to keep what they see as theirs. You don't want to go wandering around by yourself, especially at night. You are welcome to hang out here if you want to."

You see the panic in his eyes.

"You don't have to if you don't want to. I'm just offering. You do what you want, but don't come back here to steal my stuff. If you come expecting food, then you'd better get used to the idea of earning it. That means helping me go around the neighborhood and collect what we might need. If you're good with that, I'm happy to have the company. You think about it and decide."

He nods. That seems to be his preferred form of communication. As he's leaving, he says, "Thank you."

"See you tomorrow?"

He shrugs.

Huh, you think, *his language skills are expanding.*

Go to Chapter 3 on page 118

1B2a2) *What do you do now?* Your mind races, recalling every medical drama you'd ever watched. You grab scissors and cut away her shirt. You clean out the wound with bottled water and a dish towel. Blood seeps around the bullet hole. It is small and you know you'll have to make it bigger to remove the bullet. Kitchen knives won't do. You find a utility knife in the garage. You replace the razor blade with a new one to ensure it is sharp and clean. You grab your long-handled grill lighter and click the igniter, holding the blade under the flame to sterilize it.

What else? You go through the drawers until you find the box of latex gloves. You snap on a pair and try to think if there's anything else you need. You grab a roll of paper towels.

You blow out a breath and press the blade to the edge of the wound, hesitating. The thought of cutting into her sends a wave of nausea through you. *No!* You can't get sick now. Her life depends on you.

She moans, startling you. You recoil, your breathing fast and heavy. *My God!* What if she wakes up while you're slicing into her?

You run upstairs again and grab the bottle of sleeping pills. Lifting her head, you force a pill down her throat. She gags on the water, but the pill goes down. You scan the label on the bottle, wondering how long you should wait for it to take effect. You give it ten minutes before poking her in the leg a few times. No response, so you begin. The first slice sickens you. You turn away and gag on the rising bile, but force it down and return to the task. You remind yourself that this might be her only chance for survival.

You slice deeper, the layers parting like firm Jell-O under the razor. She moans and squirms. You can tell she feels it. You have to work fast before she fully awakens. You make a cut on the opposite side. Then you realize you need something to probe the wound to find the bullet, and tweezers or something to use to extract it.

Rummaging through the kitchen drawers, you find a metal skewer. You run back upstairs and locate the tweezers in a bathroom drawer. You pinch them together and study them, wondering if they will open wide enough to get around the bullet. You look at the skewer, your makeshift probe. Maybe it would be better to try and pry the bullet up. You pray that you make the right choice and she survives.

You sterilize the skewer and the tweezers with the lighter and return to your task. Whether from the probing of her tender flesh or the heat of the skewer, she moans louder. You hit something solid and blot the area with a wad of paper towels. Without constant blotting or being able to administer suction, the hole repeatedly fills with blood, making it impossible to see the bullet. At least you know where it is.

You slide the skewer around the bullet and she wakes with a scream. She rolls on her side.

Shit!

You withdraw the skewer and let her calm down. She eyes you through fat welling tears.

"You've been shot. I'm trying to remove the bullet."

She sobs and shakes her head, in too much pain to form words.

In a soft, hopefully reassuring tone, you say, "If I don't get it out, you'll die. Do you want me to try?"

The agony is too intense. She can only nod. You give her two pain pills and another sleeping pill, hoping you aren't overdosing her. She fights the effects of the sleeping pill. It is nearly thirty minutes later that her eyes close and her breathing takes on a steady rhythm.

You roll her on her stomach, take a deep breath and start again. You fumble through the procedure, alternating between swearing and praying. She wakes just as you extract the bullet. She thrashes about the table. It takes all your strength to hold her in place.

"It's over. I'm done."

She kicks and screams.

"Roll over so I can stop the bleeding."

But she is in too much pain and screaming too loudly to hear your words. All you can do is hold her down until her thrashing lessens. Eventually, you get her to roll over. You blot the wound, but it needs to be sutured.

You tell her, "Stay put. I'll be right back."

You run upstairs to find thread and a needle. Every needle in the sewing kit looks too big. You take the entire sewing kit, grab the bottle of peroxide, and hear a loud crash. Racing down the steps, you find her on the floor, face up. Her eyes are unfocused, which may be a blessing. You kneel beside her and turn her over. Blotting the hole, you pour peroxide into the wound. It bubbles and she bucks and kicks. You repeat the process until there are no more bubbles.

You wipe the wound as clean as possible, then begin stitching with white thread and a tiny needle. It is not the best patch job you've ever done, but you've never sewn skin before. You lose track of time. When you are finally finished, you back away from her, pull your knees to your chest and rock back and forth and watch her. She is no longer moving, but she does appear to be breathing.

After a while, you fix a sandwich out of whatever you can find in the kitchen. Who knows how long you'll have perishable food? You're not all that hungry, but you need to keep your strength up. You grab a bottle of water and sit in the family room. You look out the window and notice night has fallen.

After you finish eating, you place a pillow under her head and cover her with a blanket. Her breathing is shallow but steady. You offer one more silent prayer for her before you curl up on the couch and sleep.

In the morning, you find her body is cold and she is no longer breathing. You wonder if you could have done anything different to save her.

A mixture of sorrow and guilt assail you. You bend over her body and whisper. "I'm sorry."

With a surprising lack of emotion, you go outside to dig a grave.

Go to Chapter 2 page 62

1B2a3) You look at the wound. You have no idea how to save her. She is writhing on the table with an almost constant scream-gasp-moan combination. You try to comfort her with words, but have no actions to back them up.

You try to roll her over, but the agony is too great and she fights you. "I have to see the wound. I need to turn you over onto your stomach."

"It hurts. It hurts. Make it stop. Please!"

You run to get her some pain pills. Unfortunately, you have nothing stronger than that. You pick up a bottle of water and raise her head so she can swallow, but she chokes and spits the pills out. You try to think, but her screaming makes it difficult. Then you get an idea. You take two spoons from a drawer and grind the pills into powder and dump it into a glass.

You hesitate for a beat before you fill the glass with water. The woman's screams are becoming louder and longer. Her pain is unbearable to both of you. You crush four more pills into the glass and pour the water.

She downs half the water before choking and spraying it out. You lower her to the floor and get two pillows and a blanket. You put a pillow under her legs and her head, then cover her. Her wailing continues for another thirty minutes before weakening from either exertion, the pills, or approaching death; you're not sure which.

You hope she can sleep, if only to stop the screams that now echo through your head. If she sleeps, you can roll her on her side and check the wound, although you're not sure what you can do about it.

The screams lessen. She whimpers and pleads for the pain to end. Her eyes open and find you. "Please," she says, "make it stop."

Your eyes fill as you reply, "I don't know how."

Eventually, she drifts into an uneasy unconsciousness, but the moaning continues. At this point, you know she's dying. You can think of only one way to end her misery. Zombie-like, you go into the family room and pick up a throw pillow.

You stand over her. Her face, which might have been pretty once, is now twisted in agony. Smothering is the best thing…the only thing you can do for her. It will end her now-painful life. Isn't that what you would want someone to do for you?

You step closer, position the pillow over her face and stop. You can't bring yourself to do this. Then she screams again, startling you. In one motion, without thought, you plunge the pillow over her face and press it down, molding your hands over her mouth and nose. She fights for air. Muffled cries of panic seep around the edges of the pillow. It nauseates you. You want to stop. It's a mistake. There must be something else you can do, but you know the truth. With or without your aid, she is going to die. This is the only humane thing you can do for her.

Her eyes meet yours over the top of the pillow, pleading. But somewhere within them, you think you see understanding and acceptance. It may be a creation of your mind to lessen the guilt, but you'd rather believe it was something else. Her flailing subsides and she goes limp. You hold the pillow in place for another minute before lifting it.

Mouth and eyes open, she is at last at peace.

With tears in your eyes, you go outside to dig a grave.

As you pat down the last of the dirt over her, you mutter, "Congratulations! You are now a killer."

You drop the shovel and walk back to the house wondering, how many more there will be.

Go to Chapter 2 Page 62

1B2b) The scene unfolding before you is surreal. It can't be happening. There can't be very many survivors. Why does it have to come to this? There has to be enough food and water to share. How could this happen?

Afraid to move, you watch as the man stalks toward her. His eyes and the gun trained on her never waiver. Standing over her, he says something imperceptible and shoots her again. Her body jumps once and stills.

The man bends and picks up the bottled water she had been carrying. *He killed her for water?* This is wrong—no; this is crazy. Had the world gone chaotic in the last three days due to lack of authority to keep the survivors in check?

A strong feeling of guilt comes over you. You should've tried to help her. You had a chance to save her and you froze. You chastise your cowardice until the man rises, his arms full, and notices your idling car.

Shit!

He drops the bottles and they bounce at his feet. He raises the gun and advances toward you just as he'd done to the woman. Panic lances your heart. You yank the shifter into reverse and jam down on the gas. The car jerks backward as the first bullet flies toward you. More follow. You hear them impacting the car through a dense fog of your own fear.

Angling the car into a driveway, you spin the wheel hard, shift into drive and speed away. A bullet punches through the rear window and is buried into the back of the passenger seat. It is enough motivation for you to push the pedal all the way to the floor.

The man becomes smaller and smaller in your rearview mirror. Your mouth has gone dry and you realize you are breathing like you'd just run a marathon. Could you have done anything to save that woman? Probably, but you were paralyzed with fear. As you pull into the driveway, you realize if you are going to survive this new world, you are going to have to learn to protect yourself.

Go to Chapter 2 Page 62

1B2c) The man's gun is leveled at the woman. She cries out and tries to back away, but her injury prevents her from getting very far. You cannot let this man kill her. You have no weapon, but you've made up your mind to do something. As the man closes on the defenseless woman, you shift the car into drive and floor it.

He doesn't notice your approach. His undivided focus is on the woman, and it isn't until the last second that he turns toward you. You duck reflexively as he aims at you. A bullet punctures the windshield and an involuntary scream escapes your mouth. Your bladder threatens to release.

You continue to drive forward and the man fires twice more, both rounds punching through the windshield mere inches from you. You scream again, this time more as a battle cry as the car strikes the shooter. He flips onto the hood, his head shattering the windshield. You drive forward another twenty feet and brake hard. He rolls from the hood to the ground.

Heart pounding and breathing fast, you put the car in reverse. To your amazement, the man pushes to his knees, shakes his head and starts to rise.

Your eyes feel like they've been stretched impossibly wide over your face. You think about every slasher movie you've ever seen and have an urgent desire to flee. But as he regains his footing, albeit on shaky legs, you think about how he shot down the woman in cold blood. Anger pushes aside your fear. You shift into neutral, press the pedal to the floor, and shove the stick into drive. Nothing happens for several seconds as the tires squeal and spin, digging for traction. Finally, the car shoots forward, throwing you back into your seat like a fighter pilot.

The man raises the gun and you duck, the bullet tearing into the headrest where your head had been. You feel the impact, then look up. The shooter is not in sight. Then the car bounces twice, and you know he's become a human speed bump.

You brake, yanking the wheel hard to the left. The car swerves as the tires screech on the pavement. A bloody limb lies in the middle of the road. You don't feel regret or sadness. Instead, you are calm with relief. You scan the area and wait a bit before getting out of the car. Even then, you can't take your eyes from the remains of the shooter, fearing he will rise again.

Without taking your eyes from the body, you slowly walk toward the woman. Your foot hits a water bottle, telling you you've made it. You crouch next to her and check for a pulse. Nothing. With a sigh, you say a silent prayer, then gather up the bottles. You count six. Which is worse, that she was willing to risk her life for six bottles of water, or that he was prepared to kill for them?

You walk back to the car, toss the bottles on the front seat and look back at the shooter. You should go for the gun, but the memory of those same slasher movies prevents you from getting close.

You get in the car and drive away. The encounter has been beneficial in three ways: you now know you are not alone, it is an everyone-for-themselves world now, and you need to start stockpiling things to ensure your survival before others come.

You need to go home and make plans.

Go to Chapter 2 at the * * * on Page 108

1C) You decide to go through the homes of your suburban neighborhood and stock up on what you will need to continue to survive.

You grab a flashlight, a hammer, a large screw driver, two canvas shopping bags, and a chef's knife. Placing the flashlight in your back pocket and the screwdriver in your belt, you head to the neighbor's house on the right.

Several of the houses in the subdivision were built within the last five years. They are mostly two-story, four-bedroom, two-and-a-half bath residences with attached two-and-a half car garages.

You try the front door. It is locked. You insert the screwdriver tip even with the latch between the frame and the door and tap it in with the hammer. You pry it, confident you can pop it. It doesn't budge, and you remember most homes have a deadbolt, too. You back away and rethink your entry.

If you smash a window, anyone who searches around later will know someone had been here. It might be safer and easier to enter from the back. You walk around the house to the patio doors. The screen door is easy to pop and pull back. The interior door takes more work but finally gives way. You slide it open and go inside.

You haven't seen the neighbors in days. You call out a hello, but no one responds. Setting your tools down on the counter, you open the refrigerator to see if anything inside is still good. That brings up a new concern. How will you keep things cold? You could use a cooler and some ice. You check the freezer and find it is still somewhat cold and the ice is mostly melted. Still, it will work for a while.

You take an unopened carton of orange juice, a loaf of rye bread, and a bag of apples. From the freezer, you grab a pack of hot dogs and two T-bone steaks. You go through the cupboards. There is a wealth of canned and packaged food; more than will fit in the two bags you brought.

Under the sink, you find a box of garbage bags. You take one out and fill it, then open a second. By the time you're done, you have three garbage bags full of food to go with your two canvas bags. You decide it's time to lug the booty home. On the third trip, you have one last garbage bag to go. You hate to leave without going through the rest of the house, but it's already late. Do you:

1C1) go home and organize your supplies? Page 79

1C2) go through the rest of the house? Page 84

1C3) drop the last bag at home and search the next house while you have an opportunity? Page 85

1C1) You take the last bag home and see what you have. You quickly realize you might not have a place to store everything. You could stash it all in your cupboards; you have ample space, but what if other survivors come into the neighborhood in search of food? If anyone got in while you were out scavenging, everything you'd just collected would be gone.

You look at the items now spread out on the counter and feel suddenly overwhelmed. This requires more planning than you thought. You sit down and work out the details. First thing is to find a secure place for the food. The only logical choice is the basement.

You go downstairs and clear everything off the shelving units. You move all the shelves against the far wall, then pile the games and toys in a three-foot-high stack in front of the shelving units. You take all the plastic storage totes and line them up the full length of the basement, and pile as much stuff as you can on top until you have built a wall the full length of the basement that nearly reaches the ceiling.

You place a four-wheeled cart stacked with six storage bins at the far end of the wall. That gives you a movable door, though you must be careful when you open it.

Then you go upstairs to find night has fallen. You haul what you collected plus the contents of your cupboards downstairs and organize everything on the shelves. You have six four-foot-long metal units and two three-foot-long plastic ones. You grab every cooler you have and place the frozen items inside with the remaining ice from the freezer, which isn't much. You'll just have to eat what thaws out the fastest first.

By the time you finish, you feel good about your plan and are anxious to start out again tomorrow. You grab one of the steaks and grill it on the deck. The aroma makes your mouth water long before it's ready to eat. You have an apple and a glazed doughnut for dessert. It is the best meal you've had in many days.

Sleep doesn't come easy. Caught between the loss of your family and the excitement of your new goal, it is hard to shut down your mind. Morning comes too early. You wake, still feeling tired, but after a quick meal you are ready to go out scavenging. Based on what you learned yesterday, you need to make some adjustments. Do you:

1C1a) walk to the next house? Page 81

1C1b) take your son's wagon? Page 82

1C1c) drive your car? Page 83

1C1a) You go two doors down to the home of new neighbors you'd never had a chance to meet. You enter in the same fashion as before and again find a goldmine of food. You lug your treasure home but after two trips and at least two more you decide this is too much work on foot. You decide you need a better way to transport your finds, especially the farther away you go from home.

Go back and choose again.

1C1b) You drag the wagon down the sidewalk to the second house. It bounces and makes a lot of noise. That worries you; you don't want to draw attention. If anyone sees what you're doing, they will either start scavenging themselves or try to take what you have.

Still, using the noisy wagon is better than having to carry your load.

You reach the house belonging to new neighbors you had not yet met. You enter through the back door and find a large amount of food here as well. Balancing the full garbage bags on the wagon proves more difficult than you thought., You can only take two bags at a time, making a second trip necessary. You bounce the laden wagon back the same way you came. One of the bags falls, spilling half the contents. You swear and pick up as fast as you can.

Once home, you empty the wagon. There must be a better way. Each house is farther away, making the trip back longer. The wagon won't do.

Go back and choose again.

1C1c You set a nearly full box of garbage bags on the passenger seat next to your tools and two large coolers. The car offers you a lot of storage space. You might be able to raid several houses in one trip.

You go to the next house in line and pull in the driveway. You go around back and use your tools to get in. You fill two and half bags and haul them out to the car. You go back in and fill an empty bag with the still-frozen ice from the freezer and pour it in a cooler. Satisfied with your progress, you drive to the next house.

Working in this fashion, you collect from six houses before sunset. When you return home, you open the garage door manually and pull into the garage. You don't want to be outside, neither in plain view, nor in the dark. Once you close and lock the garage door, you begin the long task of lugging the day's haul to the basement and putting things away.

Done, you are too tired to cook. You fix a bologna sandwich with mustard and American cheese and grab a bag of chips.

While you eat, you ponder. The shelves are filling up fast. You've only covered seven of the perhaps one hundred fifty houses. You are going to run out of room. You need a new plan, but you're too tired to think. Right now, you need a good night's sleep, and this time it comes fast.

Go to Chapter 2 at *** Page 122

1C2) You leave what you've collected at the back door and go upstairs. At the top, you pause and listen. You don't want to surprise anyone or be taken by surprise yourself. The hallway has five doors; the one in the center is for the bathroom, and it is ajar.

The other doors are bedrooms, you assume. The two on the left, as expected, are bedrooms. You glance in, then go down the hall. The first door past the bathroom leads to a larger bedroom that is a makeshift office.

You do a quick search, but find nothing of use and move on. As soon as you open the last door, your stomach lurches. The odor assaults you in a physical attack. Gagging, you slam the door and race to the bathroom and fill the sink with vomit. You only caught a glimpse, but it was enough to see two bodies; one on the floor and one in the bed. You are no expert, but your nose tells you they've been dead for a while; casualties of the first wave of the disease, perhaps.

No matter what treasures might exist in that room, nothing is worth inhaling that stench again. You wipe your mouth and sweat-drenched brow with a towel and go back downstairs. You are too weak to continue and you don't want to go back inside, so you drag everything out to the deck and make three trips. After shelving your new items, you feel hungry, but the recent upheaval has left you uncertain about eating. You fix a peanut butter sandwich anyway, down a glass of water and go to sleep.

Your dreams turn to nightmares as you picture the two bodies reanimating and stalking you endlessly like in any good zombie movie.

Go to Chapter 2 start at *** on Page 108

1C3) After dropping off your take, you walk to the next house. It is mid-afternoon; still plenty of time, but you'll have to keep watch. You don't want to be out after dark. You reach the second house and enter the same way as you did the others. This house offers a bounty and you load three bags. It takes longer than you planned, however, and the sun is setting. You pick up two bags by their knotted ends, but moving is slow and awkward, and the bags are so full, they stretch to the point you're afraid they will tear.

You set one down and carry the other in your arms. Setting it inside your door, you go back for another. It is almost dark now. As you deposit the second bag, you ponder the risks of retrieving the last one. You decide you're being foolish. There's no one out there. You go.

You reach the house and grab the third and last bag. For whatever reason, you have overfilled this one. *Why didn't you just get a fourth bag?* You strain to carry it. You get halfway home and set the bag down to catch your breath. Standing there, you are startled by a *crash.* You freeze and try to penetrate the darkness, but see nothing.

You concentrate on what you heard. *What was that?* It sounded like glass shattering. A lot of glass. Someone else *is* out here doing the same thing you are. That thought both scares and angers you. This is your territory. You don't want to share it. You also don't want any competition.

You lift the bag again and start for home, but after five steps, the bag rips and cans of food bounce off the sidewalk, clattering and pinging on the concrete. You freeze. Do you:

1C3a) gather up what you can? Page 86

1C3b) run to your house for another bag? Page 88

1C3c) wait to see if anyone responds? Page 89

1C3a) You bend down and fill your arms with as much as you can carry. In your rush, you drop a few things. Cursing under your breath, you leave them and make a run for home. Inside, you head for the kitchen and set the cans on the counter. You go to the living room window and peer out. You don't see anyone in the dusk.

Should you risk another trip? You decide it's not worth it. You hate the idea of someone stealing your potential score, but it's not worth your life. You stand by the window for a long time. If someone is out there, you can't tell.

You try to sleep on the sofa by the front window, but you startle at every sound. As the morning light filters through the shade, you peek outside. To your relief, the cans are still there. If anyone heard the noise, they didn't spot the spilled haul.

Jumping up, you grab a new bag and race outside. You toss the last can in as you hear an engine. You search for the direction of the sound and spy movement on the next block. Grabbing the bag, you race for your house. You get inside and lock the door behind you. By the time you jump on the sofa and look out the window, you see a white van. To your dismay, it stops in front of your house. Your mind whirls.

Why did it stop here? Did they see me?

The driver's door opens and a large man with wild brown hair gets out, carrying a shotgun. He scans the streets and the houses in front of him. Then, he spots something on the ground. You crane your neck to see what has caught his attention. On the grass is a large can you missed in your haste.

He walks toward it, checking for a trap, then bends and picks it up. It has a yellow and red label. You remember the can. It's tomato sauce. You thought you might be able to make spaghetti sauce out of it, or maybe tomato soup.

The man tucks it under his arm and levels the gun. He backs away with slow, careful steps. His gaze sweeps from side to side and the gun follows as if attached to his head. He reaches the van, tosses the can inside, then climbs in and drives away.

Once he's out of sight, you try to relax, but can't. A rival has arrived, and he is armed.

Go to Chapter 2 start at *** on Page 108

1C3b) The noise paralyzes you for an instant. You look toward the noise, expecting someone to appear in the dark. Then you hear the echo of a car door slamming somewhere to the right. Whoever is out there has most likely heard you. The fear of discovery spurs you into action.

You race for the house, grab two garbage bags from the kitchen and run back out. You scan the darkness, but if anyone is out there, they're keeping their distance. Unsure of exactly where the bag broke, you keep moving forward until you kick a can. You bend and feel around, throwing whatever you find into one of the bags. You cover the flashlight with your palm to block the beam and turn it on. You pan the ground to see what else is there and pick up the majority of what you dropped as you see a cone of light on the intersecting street. Someone is coming.

Turing off your light, you run for the house and close the door just as a vehicle turns the corner. It slows as it passes your house. The headlights cast enough light for you to see it is a white van. It stops for a second in front of your house. You barely make out a shadow moving inside. Is someone searching for you?

What are you going to do if he gets out of the van?

You begin to plot your moves when the van moves on. You relax, but keep vigil at the window for a long time after it has gone.

After a while, you begin to second guess your decision to run. What if the person inside was friendly and only looking for someone to join up with? He might not have been a killer. Now you might never know.

But what if he was a killer?

Better safe than sorry. But it makes you think. You might need a weapon to protect yourself.

One thing is for sure: you are not alone, and regardless of the man's intentions, you'd better be prepared if you should meet again.

Go to Chapter 2 start at *** on Page 108

1C3c) You back away from the sidewalk and crouch behind a small white birch tree in the middle of your front yard. You don't have long to wait. Headlights shine on the intersecting street. The sound of an engine gets louder. A vehicle stops at the corner, then turns your way. As the headlights swing toward you, you realize the poor choice of hiding place you made. The cones of light will shine directly at you.

You dive to the ground and try to wiggle into the mulch. The light sweeps over you. You're sure your heart is pounding loud enough to be heard inside the vehicle. You risk a peek as the lights go past. It is a white van and you see one person in the front, but there may be others in the back.

It stops even with your house. Fear stabs your heart. The driver's door opens. You have seconds to decide. Do you:

1C3c1) get up and run? Page 90

1C3c2) stay put and risk discovery? Page 92

1C3c1) Before the driver gets around the front of the van, you push up to your feet and run, not caring as much about stealth as distance. You hear, "Hey!" and run faster. At any second, you expect to hear the pursuit of bullets or people. You turn the corner and go around the back of your house. You jump for the deck, but you catch your foot on the top stair and tumble. Pain flashes through your knee.

You hobble to the patio door, but when it doesn't slide open, you remember you locked it. *Damn!* Not sure how much time you have, you limp down the stairs and into the backyard. You trip over something and realize it's your son's grave. You crawl alongside the mound and press in tight, like you're trying to join him.

You wait for what feels like an eternity, never sure if your next breath will be your last. Then, you hear the pitch of the engine change. You lift your head, but don't see or hear any pursuit. Crawling between the houses, you see the van drive away. You wait a good five minutes before rising and creeping to the front of the house.

You squat at the corner and survey the area with your ears and your eyes. You don't hear the engine or see the headlights, but that doesn't necessarily mean they are gone. The driver could've turned around down the street and shut everything off. He might be sitting there right now, watching and waiting for you to make a move.

Unsure of what to do and not wanting to risk being out in the open, you edge along the front of the house until you reach the small front porch. There you step up, open the door and duck inside. You lock up and go to the living room window. Ducking, you pull the bottom corner of the curtain aside and peer out. You don't see anything, but unless the dome light inside the van was on, you wouldn't. On the plus side, if you can't see him, he can't see you… you hope.

You keep watch all night, dozing off a few times. Each time you startle awake, it's in a panic that you missed something.

The morning light finds you leaning against the wall asleep. You jolt awake and peer out the window. After a thorough visual search, you are confident he is gone, but unfortunately, so is everything you dropped on the sidewalk. The scavenger picked it clean.

The loss angers you. You will have to be better prepared on any future excursions. You were lucky this time.

You drag your butt to the sofa and flop down. In minutes, you're asleep.

Go to Chapter 2 start at *** on Page 108

1C3c2) Heart pounding, you watch a lone figure walk around the van and stop on the sidewalk thirty feet away. A flashlight beam pans just short of your hiding place. If you're discovered, you will have to decide whether to flee or attack. Right now, though, fear has you paralyzed.

The light stops on the pile of fallen cans.

"Well, what have we got here?"

You peek as if you don't know what he is talking about. He squats over the booty. Pulling a plastic bag from his pocket the man begins collecting. "Looky here, Dougie, ole boy; you got some beef stew and some chicken soup, and oh hell yeah, some cashews. You hit the motherlode."

You hear a bag ripping, and Ole Dougie begins chomping loudly. He licks his fingers, tongue smacking, and goes back to filling plastic bags. He pulls out bag after bag and fills four, naming each item as he slips it away.

"Gonna need me some more bags." He rises, and with the flashlight showing the way, goes back to the van. You decide that if he goes around the other side of the van, you'll make a break for it, but instead, he goes to the side closest to you and slides back the door. He deposits the full bags and pulls out a fistful of empty ones. Gathering what's left, he looks around again. "Wonder who would've dropped this and left it here. Something must've frightened them off." He shines the light on your house. "Knock, knock. Anyone home?" he cackles. "Guess I'll have to come back later and find out."

He finishes packing up and walks to the van. Securing the bags, he slides the door closed, then pans the light over the ground again. This time the light slides right over the top of you. Your heart sinks. You are ready for flight, but the light keeps moving.

"Well Dougie, ole boy, guess you got some competition in this neighborhood." He cackles again. "Not for long. No sir, not for long."

He climbs inside and drives away.

You get up and stare after the taillights. You will have to prepare better for your next excursions. No way are you going to be scared off or have your stockpile ransacked.

You go inside, sit down at the kitchen table and begin to plot.

Go to Chapter 2 start at *** on Page 108

1B1a1a2a) You try to open the door, but to your despair, it is locked. The dog scampers under the car door and snaps at you. You kick and the dog backs away, giving you just enough space to jump back into the car. You manage to get inside, but smack your head on the frame in the process. You shut the door.

The shepherd races around the car, barking. You gained nothing from the attempt, except to add a severe headache to your existing pains.

Go back and try again.

Chapter 2 from 1B1a2b2) You wake the next morning, feeling sore and slightly feverish. You take another antibiotic pill and check the wounds. Most have scabbed over, but the worst ones need more attention. You clean the wounds, blot them dry, and pour more peroxide over them. The smaller one looks good, but the larger bite bubbles up. You repeat the process twice more before drying and covering the larger wound.

The earlier night, you sat down and made a list of needs; first and foremost, being medical supplies. It's apparent to you now that this new world is more dangerous than the former, although before the catastrophic world-ending event, you wouldn't have believed that to be possible.

You make some sandwiches, and after eating, you lie back down to allow your body to recuperate, if only for a while. You are anxious to go out again. After a short nap, you prepare.

Continue on Page 108

Chapter 2

You wake to see the sun shining through the windows. Your body aches and your wounds burn. Fearful of infection, you check the bandages. Most of your wounds are dry, but two have seeped; the pads adhering to the injured area. You try to peel them back slowly, but the pain is too great, so you decide a quick rip is better. Both wounds open again. One seeps a bit, but the larger bite wound bleeds.

You press the same bandage against it to staunch the flow, but it will take more than that. Finding a kitchen towel, you tie it around the area, but it is a short towel and you can't get it tight enough. You hold it in place while searching for more medical supplies, and a few bandages and some disinfectant cream is all you find.

"What the hell? Didn't anyone ever get hurt in this house?"

You clean the wound, but the bandages are too small to cover it. The bleeding doesn't look like it will stop on its own. You need to do something.

You limp to the window and survey the area. The dogs are nowhere to be seen. You look over at your house, which is across the street and two houses to the right. You think you can make it there as long as the dogs are gone. It is decision time. Do you:

2A) stay put and rest? Page 97

2B) go home? Page 106

2A) You opt for safety. You are in no condition to outrun dogs. If you stay there, you can rest and hopefully regain some of your strength. The most important thing right now is to stop the bleeding. Running will only aggravate the injury and make recovery more difficult.

You grab a roll of paper towels and go to the couch, propping your leg up on the arm and blotting the wounded area. The blood isn't subsiding. You go through the entire roll of paper towels in only a few minutes. Somehow you need to slow the blood flow.

Getting up, you hobble to the kitchen, leaving a trail of red behind. You take a knife from the butcher block on the counter and go upstairs. Finding a sheet in the linen closet, you cut it in long strips. You go into one of the bedrooms and sit on the bed. Taking the strips, you tie the fabric around your leg and draw the strips tight. It hurts, but it's better than bleeding to death. The first strip doesn't do much, but by the third one, the wound narrows. You finish tying off the strips, then cut another six. You layer those over the top. Your leg feels tingly, like you've cut off the circulation. That's a good thing, you decide, and cut more strips. By the time you've cut up the entire sheet, there's a large mound wrapped around your leg. For the moment, you don't see any blood spotting through.

Placing a pillow under your leg, you lie back and close your eyes. *Damn!* You should've looked for pain pills. You don't want to get up and start the blood flowing again, so you push the thought aside and go to sleep.

You toss and turn as strange, extremely vivid nightmares invade your subconscious. You wake with a gasp and sit up. You're confused by your surroundings. The answer comes slowly. Your leg burns and your face is covered with perspiration. You wipe your face with a pillow and feel your forehead. You are burning up. At the very least, one of your wounds is infected.

You need to find something to bring the fever down, so you get out of bed. As soon as you put weight on your legs, pain shoots from your knee all the way up your body. You cry out and lean back to take the weight off.

Damn!

Now you're sure which wound it is, as if you had any doubt. The big one is painful to the touch as you probe it with your fingers. You hop and drag your injured leg to the bathroom. Tearing through the drawers, you find three bottles of pain pills. You read the labels to determine which might offer the best relief, and down three.

You need to find some sort of antibiotic or you may die. You do a thorough search of the bathroom. Coming away empty, you hop to the stairs, sit down and slide down on your butt. You move to the kitchen and scour the drawers and cabinets but find nothing.

You think there might be a few of your son's prescription pills left. Probably not many, but you will take what you can get.

Your thigh is throbbing, but you're not sure if it's because the bandages are too tight or because of the infection. Most likely, both.

You move to the rear door and peer out. The distance isn't that great. You're sure you can make it. You reach for the door, then freeze. Movement outside the fence grabs your attention. You narrow your gaze. There, behind a tree, is the German shepherd. It is sitting perfectly still, eyes focused your direction.

"What the hell...? Is this the Einstein of dogs?"

How are you going to get past it? You must do something. The longer you wait to take antibiotics, the worse the infection will become. The same choice presents itself. Do you:

2A1) try for home? Page 102

2A2) wait out the dog? Page 105

1B1a1a2b) You rest for a while and wait for the dog to settle before making a move. But since the door is locked, you need a different way to get inside. You remember how you got into your house from the garage once when you'd locked yourself out.

You pull out your wallet. Why you still carry it, you don't know; maybe out of habit, but you're glad you do. You pull out a Visa card and stare at it. One good thing about the current situation is not having to pay off the balance. You hesitate as another thought comes to you. Just in case, you slide it back in its pocket and instead withdraw an old department store charge card that has no balance. You are tired and force yourself physically and mentally to move.

The dog is in the same spot, but now sitting instead of sleeping. You pull the handle as quietly as possible, but there's no hiding the noise once you open the door. This time, you stretch your foot toward the shelving unit.

The dog charges. You snag the support post and pull. It is heavier than you'd anticipated because of everything piled on top, but it does move, scraping on the cement floor. A second tug closes off the space beneath the car door. You yank once more to snug the barrier in place.

The shepherd stops running, but continues to bark a constant cacophony. The other dogs, though still outside, hear the shepherd and add their own tones to the symphony.

Putting your shoulder into the door, you slide the card next to the latch. You push and shove and curse as the anxiety builds. Several long seconds later, you are rewarded with a whoosh of air as the door gives way. You slam the door shut behind you and collapse against it, heart pounding like a jack hammer.

As the adrenaline drains from your system, it leaves pain; all-encompassing pain.

Unable to form thoughts for a long while, you sit and stare at the wall. A thump against the barrier at the patio door snaps you from your fugue. Your vision clears and you focus on a row of hooks attached to the wall, but not so much the hooks as what is hanging from them. Car keys.

A rush of excitement invigorates you as a quick plan forms, but it all depends on where the shepherd is. You get up and hobble toward the keys. Your inflamed wounds and stiffened muscles make moving difficult and painful. You find three sets of keys, but there is only one car in the garage.

Each set has a fob. You open the door a crack and press the unlock buttons on each one. The first and third set both work for the car. You see a garage door opener attached to the ceiling. With no electricity, you'll need to open the door manually, which means you'll have to face the shepherd again.

As if somehow reading your thoughts, the shepherd growls. You close the door.

Your eyes light on a frying pan. You stand behind the door and open it, hoping the dog will run inside and you can duck out, but of course, that doesn't happen. You peek into the garage and although you hear the growling, you don't see the dog.

As fast as your wounded body allows, you step into the garage and make your way to the rear of the car. The sound of scrabbling on the cement floor tells you the shepherd is in motion. You step up the bumper and climb on the trunk just as the dog jumps up, snapping at your heels. It finds no purchase, but you don't want to give it a chance. You swing the pan and it ducks out of the way.

Standing on the trunk, you reach the overhead door release. Hand over hand, grabbing the metal panels, you lift the door. Seeing the daylight pouring in, the shepherd runs out. It turns and faces you, barking ferociously.

You jump down and the dog sprints at you. Panic rises once more. You fling the pan at it and jump into the passenger seat, shutting the door before the dog can get to you. It stands on hind legs and leans against the passenger window, barking non-stop.

You settle into the driver's seat, insert the key and are about to turn it when a large dog jumps against the driver's side window. Your heart skipping a beat, you scream in shock. You twist the key with a silent prayer as the engine turns over.

Without a hesitation, you jam the stick into reverse and floor it. The car bounces over a doggy speed bump. You are down the driveway in seconds, dogs following. You shift into drive, flip the dogs off and head for home. For a while, a small pack chases the car, and you fear they will chase you all the way home. Soon the numbers dwindle and only the shepherd pursues.

That dog sure must have hated its owner.

A few quick turns and increased speed, and you lose the dog… you hope. You park in front of the house, find your house keys in a pocket, and scan the premises. Still no dogs. You get out and limp as fast as you can to the house, unlock the door, and get inside. Safe. You lock the doors and go about tending to your injuries. You wonder if it will ever be safe to leave the house again.

It is then you determine that to survive, you'll need a much better plan than to just wander aimlessly. You find an antibiotic prescription that your son never finished and swallow one of the pills, hoping it will help with any infection. With your wounds cleansed and bandaged, you sit down and prop your leg up on a pillow and begin making a list of things you'll need.

Go to Chapter 2 Page 108

2A1) You decide that if you don't go home and get those antibiotics in you soon, you will die a horrendous death. You're not going to let that dog stop you. You go to the kitchen and grab the biggest chef's knife you can find. You heft it. The weight gives you confidence, but as you move, you become unsure of yourself. You might have a weapon, but you have no mobility. What if there are more dogs out there that you can't see? You won't stand a chance. But to stay is to die anyway, so it's better to try something.

Slow and quiet is your plan. You inch the patio door open, keeping your eyes on the dog sentinel. At first, you see no response, but as soon as you step outside, the shepherd's ears go erect and its head lifts. You freeze, hoping it didn't notice you, but when the low rumble of its growl reaches you, it's time to move.

You limp toward the gate. The dog rises and glares at you; its fur bristles and its lips curl back, exposing the teeth. You swallow hard and keep moving. Reaching the gate, you lift the latch and pull it inward, using it as a shield and sandwiching you between the fence and the gate.

The shepherd races forward, but doesn't enter the yard. Instead, it tries to bite you through the fence. You step forward, luring it. It snaps at the fence, catching the metal its powerful maw. Somehow, you have to entice it into the yard. The only way to do that, however, is to offer yourself as bait.

You push the gate and step from cover. Sticking your good leg through the opening, you wiggle it like you're doing the hokey pokey.

"Here it is, you big dummy. Come take a bite."

The shepherd moves faster than you expected. It is through the gate and almost on you before you can shut the gate, trapping yourself in the corner. It tries to shove its muzzle into the gap between the gate and the fence. You pull it tight and slash out with the knife. You strike it, but just enough to evoke a yelp. The dog jumps back and eyes you with suspicion.

"Yeah, that's right. I've got a bite now, too."

You jab, but are just out of reach. Still, the dog dances back.

This time, you shout a warrior's cry, stab at the shepherd and push the gate in one motion. The dog jumps back, giving you enough room to exit the gate and close it behind you. You latch it and without hesitation, turn for home.

The shepherd begins barking and tries to jump the fence. As you hit the street and hurry toward home, answering barks erupt from everywhere in the neighborhood. Your leg is on fire as you push harder.

You cross the street and angle across the neighbor's yard. On the right, two dogs approach at a run. Other dogs bark in pursuit. You dare not look back, but in your mind's eye, you envision them a few short feet away from pouncing on you.

You reach your front yard and realize you do not have the keys in hand and ready. *Dumb ass.* You shift the knife to your left hand while snaking your right into your pocket. By some strange trick of your imagination, the pocket is smaller and tighter than ever before.

You manage to wiggle your fingers inside and wrap them around a key. Extracting them on the run proves to be difficult. Then, you notice the dogs have substantially closed the distance. The keys magically appear in your hand. You reach the door, fumble for the right key, and drop the knife.

Forcing as much calm as humanly possible given the circumstances, you line up the key with the lock and slam it home. With the first lock open, you attempt the deadbolt, but miss. Trying to forget about the dogs and concentrate, you guide the key carefully into the slot like a virgin on his wedding night. A quick twist, a firm push and you're inside—but so is one of the dogs. You slam the door in the face of the second one and are rewarded with a solid thud.

The dog is having trouble getting a grip on the wooden floor and slides into the stairs. Before it can right itself, you plant your good foot and deliver a savage kick that snaps the dog's head back and sends molten lava up your leg.

You scream, clutch at your leg, and fall against the wall. As the pain subsides, you see the dog, a mutt of some sort, is regaining clarity. You rush forward, grab it by the collar and drag it through the kitchen. You pitch the beast outside through the patio door.

You breathe raggedly until the pain lessens. Then, you hobble to the kitchen cabinet and search for the prescription bottle. You find it. Amoxicillin, and there are four pills left. You twist off the cap, grab a bottle of water and swallow the pill. Then you take two aspirin and go into the family room to lie down.

Exhausted, it doesn't take long for sleep to claim you.

Chapter 3

You are in no condition to do anything the next day. You rummage through the cupboards and find a prescription bottle with a few antibiotic pills that your son never finished. You swallow one and debate on doubling the dosage, but decide against it to make them last for as long as possible. You sit down and make a list of items you will need to survive, writing ANTIBIOTICS and underlining the word at the top of the page.

Create your own list of necessary items and compare them to the one on Page 209

Go to *** on page 133

2A2) The fever continues to spike. You feel faint and sit down and rest your head on the table. The coolness feels good. You lose track of time. When clarity comes again, you see the dog still on duty. Confident it will leave soon, you get up and take three more pain pills. You feel somewhat better and decide you just need more sleep.

You lie down on the couch in the family room. The fever takes you under; your dreams are troubled. Once, you wake to see the sun setting, but you have no strength to rise. You last another night before the damage to your system is too severe and your body can no longer fight off the infection raging within you. You drift off into another fevered state, but this time you don't wake up.

End

2B) You must take care of the major wound before it gets infected and costs you your leg, if not your life. In case you should run into the dogs again, you limp into the attached garage in search of a weapon. You find an aluminum baseball bat and heft it. It has enough weight to be deadly.

You scan the area behind the house. It still looks clear. You remove the keys from your pocket, open the door and step out. Since the enclosed yard offers security, you take your time getting to the fence. You'll need all your strength and energy for the dash across the street.

Looking both ways, you open the gate and step out of the backyard. You leave the gate open in case there is need for a fast retreat. You venture with caution into the street. Once you step onto the asphalt, you're in the open and have little chance of getting back to safety. Your mind already made up, you move as fast as your injured leg allows. You clear the street and start across the neighbor's front yard.

With a lot and a half to go, you hear the barking start. They are coming, but you don't want to risk slowing down to look back. You reach your property and head for the front porch. You envision the pack right behind you. You reach the porch, surprised they haven't attacked yet.

Yanking open the storm door, you risk a peek. They are coming toward you from all directions and zeroing in on your location. The two closest are only ten feet away.

You insert the key and open the first lock. Not sure if you have time to unlock the deadbolt, you whip around as the dogs arrive. The bat is a blur and connects with the first dog, knocking it sideways into the second. You focus on the lock. You get the key into the lock, but a glance shows you don't have enough time to enter.

You swing the bat again as two more dogs join the attack. Groping blindly with one hand, you reach behind you and feel for the keys. Turning them, you feel the door loosen in the frame. You grope once more, push the door open, and stagger in, slamming it shut behind you and manage to keep the dogs out.

The keys are still dangling in the lock, but you can get them later.

Locking the door, you go to the kitchen. You find the antibiotics and swallow one with a bottled water and go upstairs. In your bedroom, you cut a sheet into long strips. You get two gauze pads and the bottle of peroxide, then carefully peel off the soiled bandages.

You douse the wound with the peroxide. You hiss in pain and watch as the liquid bubbles. The extra runs down your leg. You repeat the process until it no longer bubbles, then blot it dry. You spread triple antibiotic ointment over the wound and cover it with the fresh pads, securing them with the strips of material, and squeeze the wound shut as best you can. Done, you lie back on the bed, prop up your leg and sleep.

Go to Chapter 3 page 104

Chapter 2

You are feverish and achy when you wake. Your body is stiff and hesitates to respond to your command to rise. Movement elicits moans. You manage to make it to the bathroom and find the thermometer. It reads a hundred and one. *Damn!* You have an infection. It's not too bad yet, but left unchecked, it will get worse, and without medical assistance, you will die.

You remember that your son didn't finish his round of antibiotics for a sinus infection. You yelled at him at the time, but now, you are thankful. You're not sure if it will work on your infection, but something is surely better than nothing, right?

You make a long and painful descent down the stairs to the kitchen. The prescription bottle is in a cabinet. Four pills remain. You take one with a long drink of water, then scrounge for food. You open a can of chicken noodle soup and eat it cold. Then you sit down in the family room and stare at the TV out of habit, not realizing—or maybe not caring—that the screen is black. You sit mindless for a long time before snapping out of your fugue.

* * * (start here from pages 76, 84, 87, 88, 91 and 93)

You should probably get some rest, but from the lessons you learned yesterday, you want to use your downtime to your advantage. You get a pen and pad of paper and sit at the dining room table, your injured leg propped on a chair.

For several minutes, you organize your thoughts, then you begin to make a list of items you will need in order by category. The list gets longer the more you think about it.

Make your own list of basic needs, then compare it to the one on page 209.

After you finish, you make breakfast outside on the grill. You use all six of the eggs, all the remaining bacon, and the last four slices of bread. No sense letting it to go waste. Might as well eat it while it's still good.

The aroma rises and you inhale deeply. Your mouth waters. This is the best meal you've had in days, if not the best ever. With the food ready, you shut down the gas, then realize you forgot to bring out a plate and utensils. You go inside to retrieve them, and when you go back to the patio door, you see a boy of about ten or twelve years old bending over the grill, grabbing your bacon. Do you:

2A) chase the boy away? Page 110

2B) sneak up and grab the boy? Page 114

2C) speak to him? Page 121

2A) Anger flashes and a red mist clouds your vision. The sight of someone eating—no, stealing your food makes you want to lash out. You step through the doorway, shouting obscenities, and plant a foot on the boy's butt. He is propelled into the grill. You hear a sizzle and the boy screams, dropping the bacon and clutching his seared hand.

"Beat it, you thief," you say and threaten to kick him again.

"But I only want something to eat. I'm starving."

"Then stop whining and go somewhere else. You can't have mine."

The boy is crying, waving his hand in hopes the air will cool it off.

"Put some ointment on it and get off my property."

You lift your leg to kick him again and he leaps from the deck, sobbing. He runs four yards down and disappears around the side of a house. You didn't see if he went inside, you make a mental note to remember him when you go over there to clean it out.

Congratulations. It only took you *how many* days to lose your humanity?

You look at the bacon that fell on the deck and sigh. You only have two slices left on the grill, and there must be eight on the deck. Do you:

2A1) use the sixty-second rule and pick up the bacon? Page 111

2A2) kick the bacon off the deck and onto the ground? Page113

2A1) "One-minute rule," you say, and bend to pick up the bacon. You wipe it all off with a paper towel and pronounce it clean enough to eat. You fill your plate with the food and go inside. You think about the boy, but only for a moment.

"Try to steal my food, will ya?" you grunt a laugh and shove a piece of bacon in your mouth. It crunches and you savor the grease and hickory flavor. You devour your meal as if you expect the boy to return at any second to fight you for it. As you swallow the last bite, you sit back, rub your belly and belch loudly.

You give a guilty glance at your spouse's grave. "Sorry," you say, knowing she wouldn't have approved, then belch louder and laugh. "Compliments to the cook." You laugh again and clean the dishes.

Making sure all the doors are locked, you go upstairs and lie down for a nap. You wake a few hours later, still feeling a bit feverish. You take the next pill, and although you feel antsy and want to get outside to start collecting, in the end, you decide your leg could use a lot more rest. You don't want to rip off the scab.

You add a few items to the list, then go downstairs to the basement, taking one step at a time. Since you're not going collecting today, you can rearrange your stockpile. You want things organized, but you also want to protect what you have from any intruders.

Making a mental note of what you have and what needs to go, you dig in. It takes the rest of the day, but you feel elated and accomplished.

It's time for the next dose of antibiotics. You then head upstairs to bed. Regardless whether your leg feels better or not, you cannot sit and waste more time. Tomorrow you will work as long as you can to fill up your shelves.

Chapter 3

You get up and organize your supplies and tools for the days collecting. Before driving away, you scan the area for the boy. He is nowhere in sight. A feeling of paranoia that he will return and wipe out your stores befalls you. You stop for a moment and ponder solutions to the problem, but can't come up with anything. It will take more thought. You hope that in time, the two of you can reach some accommodation; otherwise, you might be forced to hunt him down.

Go to *** on page 133

2A2) You sigh at the sight of the bacon on the deck, then you push it off with your foot. You still have two pieces left. You turn the grill back on to heat up the eggs, then shut it down and take your meal inside. You eat while pondering your list. You think of a few more items to add, then clean up.

You don't want to risk tearing your wound open, so you decide to work in the basement to get it ready for what you hope will be a huge haul the next day. By midday, you are exhausted. You take the next dose of antibiotic, then go upstairs to nap.

Three hours later, you wake and check your bandages. The wounds are all scabbed over, except for the big one. The jagged edge is an angry red. Too much meat is missing for it to heal over. You'll have a divot in your leg and a great story, though.

You pour more peroxide into the wound, paying special attention to the edges. It burns, but doesn't bubble like it did the previous day. Maybe it is healing. After you change the bandages, you change your shirt and pants, then go downstairs to get something done.

You eat again, then get a gym bag and stuff it with items you want to take with you tomorrow. You've done all you can for now. Tomorrow will be a big day.

Chapter 3

You get up and organize your supplies and tools for the days collecting. Before driving away, you scan the area for the boy. He is nowhere in sight. A feeling of paranoia that he will return and wipe out your stores befalls you. You stop for a moment and ponder solutions to the problem, but can't come up with anything. It will take more thought. You hope that in time, the two of you can reach some accommodation; otherwise, you might be forced to hunt him down.

Go to *** on page 133

2B) You tiptoe out onto the deck. The boy stiffens, as if his personal space radar goes off. Before he can turn or bolt, you get your arm around his neck and pull him in close.

"Trying to steal my food, eh?"

"I'm sorry. I was hungry."

"Did it occur to you that I might be, too?"

"I'm sorry. Let me go. Please!"

"Why didn't you just ask if you could have some?"

He struggled against the arm around his neck. "Because I didn't know if I could trust you."

You can't hold him there forever. What should you do with him? On one hand, you don't want the responsibility of having to look after a kid; but on the other, it might be nice to have company. Someone to talk to other than yourself. Do you:

2B1) release your hold on him and chase him off? Page 115

2B2) release your hold on him but ask him to stay? Page 116

2B3) snap his neck. Page 119

2B1) "I'm gonna let you go. Take two pieces of bacon and a slice of toast. Go and don't come back."

You release him and he eyes you with suspicion and fear. He takes what you offered and goes to the edge of the deck. He turns, thanks you, then runs down the stairs. As you watch him go, you guess you'll have to deal with him one way or another, at some point.

You finish your meal, thinking about the boy before switching gears and focusing on your list. You add a few items and figure it will grow as you go. After cleaning up and changing the bandages, you decide you need one more day to rest. You head downstairs to organize your shelves for the haul you plan on making the next day.

Chapter 3

You get up and organize your supplies and tools for the day's collecting. Before driving away, you scan the area for the boy. He is nowhere in sight. A feeling of paranoia that he will return and wipe out your stores befalls you. You stop for a moment and ponder solutions to the problem, but can't come up with anything. It will take more thought. You hope that in time, the two of you can reach some accommodation; otherwise, you might be forced to hunt him down.

Go to *** on page 133

2B2) "I'm gonna let you go. If you want to stay and share the meal with me, you're welcome to, but if you ever sneak up on me again to steal something, I won't be nice at all. Understand?"

The boy nods.

You release him and back away. If he decides to run, you want to let him know he's free to go. He rubs his neck and faces you. You study each other, then you go to the grill, plate some food and hand it to him.

"Sit down and eat. I'll get a second plate."

You leave him on the deck, but watch him through the kitchen window. Although he eyes the bacon, he makes no attempt to snatch any extra. You feel good about your decision.

Outside, you sit across the patio table from him. He is all but a few bites from finishing.

"You must've been starved."

He nods and shovels the last forkful into his mouth. Even before he swallows, he is eyeing your plate. You smile and lean further over your food, just in case.

"Still hungry?"

He nods.

You motion with your head. "Inside there's a bag of apples on the counter. Take a couple."

His eyes swing toward the house, then back to you. He wants the food, but is trying to decide if it's a trick to lure him inside.

"Go. I'm not gonna hurt you. They'll go bad if they aren't eaten soon."

He takes the chance, and seconds later is back, an apple in each hand. He bites into one with a loud crunch. The juice runs down his chin and he wipes it away with a dirty sleeve.

"What's your name?" you ask.

"Andy."

"Andy, I'm Larry (or whatever name you chose). I'm glad to meet someone else alive who's not trying to kill everyone they see. This is sure a crazy world we live in now."

The boy chomps around the apple like it's an ear of corn.

"I take it you haven't eaten in a while."

He shakes his head.

"Which house do you live in?"

He hesitates. His eyes widen and he slows his chewing.

"Hey, I'm not going to rob you or anything. I'm just curious. You're free to leave here and go home whenever you want. I only want to know which one is yours so I don't take your things. I'll skip your house." Having eaten the whole apple except for the seeds and the stem, Andy tosses what little core there is far into the yard. He polishes the second apple on his shirt and starts in on that one.

"I live four houses down."

You know the house, but you had never met Andy or his parents.

"You moved in recently, right?"

He nods again.

"Okay, look, I don't know how much you know about what's been going on, but it's really crazy out here. I've only seen one other living person and a few animals, but they are ready to kill to keep what they see as theirs. You don't want to go wandering around by yourself, especially not at night. You are welcome to hang out here if you want to."

You see the panic in his eyes.

"You don't have to if you don't want to. I'm just offering. You do what you want, but don't come back here to steal my stuff. If you come expecting food, then you'd better get used to the idea of earning it. That means helping me go around the neighborhood and collect what we might need. If you're good with that, I'm happy to have the company. You think about it and decide."

He nods. That seems to be his preferred form of communication. As he's leaving, he says, "Thank you."

"See you tomorrow?"

He shrugs.

Huh, you think, *his language skills are expanding.*

Chapter 3

You leave the house later than intended. Having stayed up late to put your collected items away, you overslept. You feel better about survival on a short-term basis, but don't want to leave it to chance. Having gone through more than a dozen houses now, you understand just how much work is ahead of you. You also know that time is an enemy. Food will rot and others will come.

Andy doesn't show up, but you're not surprised. Maybe he'll come around later, but if not, you're used to going it alone. You look for him as you drive to the first house.

Go to *** on Page 133

2B3) You sneak up behind him. He stiffens, sensing your approach, and you pounce. You slide an arm around his neck and pull the bacon from his hands. You hold it up in front of him. "You stealing from me, you little thief?" You toss the greasy slices back on the grill. "We can't have thieves around here. I work too hard collecting this food so I can survive. I can't have some young punk taking what's mine."

You grip his head and twist hard. The crack is audible, his weight suddenly heavy in your arms. You drag him down the deck and into the yard next door. You open the patio door, haul him inside and toss the body down the basement stairs.

You feel no guilt over killing him, nor does it bother you that he might have been one of the few survivors. He stole from you—and needed to be punished.

Your eyes fall on your spouse's grave and your steps falter for a moment. Then, you push memories of her aside and continue on. You are a killer now, but rationalize that's what you need to be to survive in this new cold, hard world.

You turn the grill back on for a minute to warm your food, then sit down to eat, the boy and his death no longer a concern.

Chapter 3

You have a new, more hardened approach to your existence when you wake. You slept fitfully, dreaming about your spouse and the thief. The guilt morphed into anger and you walled off the memory. You have work to do if you plan to survive, and it's time to get to work.

You skip breakfast, gather your tools and supplies and get on the road. As you drive, tears well. You are so surprised by the bottled-up emotion that you are forced to stop. The tear fall, blurring your vision.

Lifting your eyes heavenward, you say to your spouse, "Forgive me." Then to the boy, "I'm so sorry." You realize you are not the apocalyptic hard ass you think yourself to be. You can't change what you've done, but vow it won't happen again. You will only react with violence when you have no other choice.

You drive on in hopes of finding some way to atone for the murder of an innocent boy, if that is possible at all.

Go to *** on Page 133

2C) In a soft voice and nonthreatening tone, you say, "You're welcome to join me."

The boy jumps. His eyes flicker from the bacon to you, perhaps weighing his chance of a successful grab and go.

"It's okay, I'm not gonna hurt you. If you're hungry, take some. But next time, ask me—don't steal. I'm happy to share. You want me to get you a plate?"

He eyes you suspiciously, but his fear can't stop his tongue from licking his lips.

"Here," you pull out a patio chair. "Take a seat and I'll get you a plate and silverware."

You go inside and give him an opportunity to feel safe about sitting. You come back with a plate and fork, only to find him gone, having also taken the bacon and the toast. You sigh, happy he didn't want the eggs.

Chapter 3

You get up and organize your supplies and tools for the day's collecting. Before driving away, you scan the area for Andy. He is nowhere in sight. A feeling of paranoia that Andy will return and wipe out your stores befalls you. You stop for a moment and ponder solutions to the problem, but can't come up with anything. It will take more thought.

Go to *** on page 133

Chapter 2

You sleep long. You check the bandages around your thigh. Your injuries appear to be healing, though the two deeper puncture wounds still look raw and wet.

You fix the last of your eggs and bacon and toast on the grill outside on the deck. Putting everything together into a sandwich, you sit at the patio table and write down some of the things you will need to survive. You list the categories. Food. Drink. Weapons. Medical. Miscellaneous. You want to concentrate on the basics for now, leaving off equipment like a generator. Then you go about filling it in. Much of it comes to mind with ease. It is common sense, but after a while you hit a wall and need a break.

Create your own list, then check it against the one on Page 209.

With the list done for now, you go down to the basement and begin clearing room for what you'll collect tomorrow. You know you're wasting time sitting at home when others might already be out there collecting, but you're afraid of breaking your wounds open. Besides, by the time you finish remodeling the basement, it's near dark.

You fix another meal, then go to bed.

***

The morning finds you sore but rested. You check your wounds and are happy to see none are bleeding. With fresh bandages in place, it's time to get moving. After loading a gym bag with some tools, you grab your shopping list, get in the car and drive down the street to where you left off.

You park in the driveway and go around back. Breaking in is easy and you've come up with a good plan for searching each house thoroughly and efficiently in a timely manner. Because of its high value content, the kitchen is first. You load your bags and leave them near the front door. Next, you go through the garage to find tools and filled gas cans.

Then, it's upstairs to search the bathrooms for medical supplies. The bedrooms are last. Once the second floor is finished, you check out the basement. After you've been everywhere inside, it's time to load the car. You take your tool bag out first and scan the area for intruders. You place it on the front seat, then open the rear doors and trunk. You take four loads.

On your final trip, you take a last look around to see if you've missed anything, and your eyes fall on the grill on the deck. You take the last bag to the car, close the trunk and the doors, then run through the house to pull the propane tank off the grill.

You feel good about your haul as you drive to the next house, but know you won't be able to get any more than two houses' worth of supplies in the car. You're gonna need a bigger vehicle.

After clearing the second house, you go home. Not wanting to unload and waste the daylight, you drive into the garage and close the door. You grab your tool kit and run down the street to the next house in line. The first thing to do is find a larger vehicle at one of the houses and locate the key.

You open three houses without searching them. Your primary goal right now is the vehicle. At the first house, there are two smaller cars, but you need something along the lines of a large SUV, pickup, or van. The second house yields a Suburban, and not only are the keys nowhere to be found, but there is a body in it. The stench alone makes it untouchable, even if you knew how to hot wire a car.

In the third house, you find the bodies of a man and a woman sprawled on the kitchen floor. It is the man that draws your attention. He is wearing a cable company uniform. Pressing some napkins to your nose and mouth, you go to the front window and look out. You have no idea why you didn't notice it before, but parked on the street is a white van with the cable company's logo on the side.

You creep up on his body, afraid it will rise from the floor. Fighting down the rising bile, you search his pockets until you find the key.

"Yes!"

You run outside, start the van and back it up the driveway. You open the overhead door of the garage and unload the van of all unnecessary items as fast as you can. Returning to the house, you make a search and bag your findings. After loading the van, you drive back to the other two houses you opened but did not loot.

It is in the third house where you find the one item on your list you starred as an absolute must-find. A 9mm Sig Sauer P226. It's in a case on the shelf in a bedroom closet. The box contains two magazines, both empty. Next to the gun case is a small cardboard box holding bullets and a cleaning kit. The fifty-count box is missing thirteen rounds, or what you estimate to be one magazine's worth.

You are excited by your find and feel confident to have it on your person. You sit on the bed and load both magazines, then place one in your pocket and one in the gun. You've shot before, but you are far from being an expert. You examine the gun and find the safety. You rack a round into the chamber and feel ready, but as a precaution to make sure you don't shoot yourself, you reset the safety.

The day goes fast. The van allows you to search a lot more houses and stow the loads with no trips back to your house. By the fourth one, you've got your routine down pat.

You're on your way upstairs when you hear a thud. You freeze, your hand instinctively touching the butt of the gun stuck in the back of your pants. You listen and think you hear a footstep. Your first instinct is to retreat and sneak out, but having the gun emboldens you. You pull it out and flick off the safety. You hear it again. It's coming from the right. You step into the hall and creep forward, the floor creaking under your second step. You pause, angry to have possibly announced your presence. You calm your breathing, but your heartbeat continues to race.

You reach the door, which is shut. You lean forward and put your ear to the wood. You're unsure if you truly did hear anything. It could have been fear-induced imagination. You release the gun and grab the doorknob. Turning it slowly, you try to decide the best way to enter. You opt to fling the door open and duck back rather than rush right in.

The latch clears and the door gives. You take a few quick breaths, then fling it open. You duck back just as something pings off the wall behind you. You had a quick glimpse of someone standing in a shooter's stance on the far side of the room next to the bed.

Do you:

2A) run? Page 126

2B) shoot? Page 127

2C) call out? Page 129

2A) Having a gun is one thing, but having someone shooting at you is something completely different. You dash across the doorway and sprint down the stairs. Ignoring the full bags by the door, you bolt out, hop in the car and drive home.

You hop out and raise the overhead door and drive into the garage. Closing the door behind you, you go inside the house and sit down. It is a good hour before your body stops trembling. Having a gun doesn't do you any good if you're too afraid to stand up to someone else with a gun.

On the other hand, you rationalize that he who runs away lives to collect another day.

You keep a vigil at the window deep into the night. Whoever was shooting at you might have followed, but after night fell, you stopped your watch. If he was coming, you'd never see him. Sleep however, did not come easy. Every sound had you sitting up in bed. When you woke in the morning, you felt like you hadn't slept at all.

Chapter 3

You fortify yourself with a good breakfast, then draw in your courage and go out again. This time, you choose an area away from the shooter's house. You approach each house with more caution. The gun is at the ready in your hand. Fortunately, you have no need for it and soon relax.

Yesterday's gunfire has left you edgy and you change up your routine. You clear the house first before collecting. It makes the process slower but safer.

Go to *** on page 133

2B) You line up your shot from the doorway, aim the gun and pull the trigger, but nothing happens. You stand there like a dumbass, staring at the gun. Another shot pings off the wall, nipping at your ear as it passes. You cry out, more from the shock than the pain. It stings, but you can function.

You duck to the right and press against the wall. Again, you look at your gun, wondering why it didn't fire. You did everything right. You remembered the safety. What were you forgetting?

You think about the shooter. Why had his shot sounded so strange? Was he using a suppressor? You look at the wall and see two small holes. Are bullets that tiny? They look so much bigger in the box.

You debate if you should flee or stay. You study the gun, then cock the trigger. It locks in place. Without looking, you poke it through the door and pull the trigger. This time, it fires. The gun bucks at the awkward angle and flies upward and almost out of your grip.

So, that's it, you think, *I have to cock it first.*

You cock it again and calm your breathing, then jump in front of the doorway. You aim at your target, finger pressing the trigger, then stop. The shooter is not there. You feel the stranglehold of panic constricting your throat. *Where the hell is he?*

You pan the room, looking down the sights. You see a foot sticking out from under the far side of the bed. Keeping your gun trained on a spot above it over the edge of the bed where you think the shooter might pop up, you enter the room.

"Throw your gun out and I won't shoot you."

No response.

You become more nervous and notice the gun trembling in front of you. You take another step. Sweat runs down your nose. You try to blow it away. You repeat your demand, but again, no reply. Another step. *Is it a trap?* Your hands are shaking so bad, you doubt you can hit anything but the wall.

You angle far enough away from the bed to be able to see along the side. You see the torso, then the gun still in his hand. He doesn't appear to be breathing, but again, it could be a trick. You step closer and kick at his foot.

"Hey! Throw down the gun. Don't make me shoot you." To yourself, you add, "Please!"

One more step gives you a clear look at the shooter. There is a small hole in his forehead, just above the left eye. You're shocked; you can't believe the lucky shot. But what shocks you even more is recognizing the face. It's Andy, the boy who tried to steal your bacon.

In an instant, you are on the floor, heaving and vomiting. You crawl away and sit against the wall. Your body is shaking. You feel sick again, but nothing else comes up.

As the urge subsides, you get up and go into the hallway bathroom. You wipe your mouth on a towel and stare at the red eyes that glare back at you from the mirror. They're now the eyes of a killer; nothing will ever be able to change that.

No longer in the mood to search and collect, you load up the bags you've already filled and drive home. Once inside the house, you collapse in a chair and curl in the fetal position. You killed a boy. A boy only a few years younger than your own son had been.

The tears come and you let them fall.

Chapter 3

You leave the house later than intended, having stayed up late to dig a grave for the boy. After you wake you put away the items you collected the night before. You were too depressed to do it last night.

You feel better about your short-term survival, now that you have some food and supplies, but you don't want to leave it to chance. Having gone through more than a dozen houses now, you understand just how much work is ahead of you. You also know that time is an enemy. Food will rot and others will come.

Go to *** on page 133

2C) "Don't shoot. I don't want to hurt you."

No response.

"Talk to me. Let's not shoot each other for no reason."

"Then get the hell out of my house."

The voice sounds young and somehow familiar. It comes to you in a rush. "Hey, you're the kid who stole my bacon."

"Yeah, so what?"

"So, nothing. I didn't know this was your house. I'm leaving. Don't shoot me as I go. I will be forced to shoot back." You wait, but he doesn't say anything else. "Hey! You hear me? I'm leaving. I apologize for breaking into your house. I'll leave everything downstairs." You duck and leap across the doorway. "Don't shoot, now. I'm leaving. If you ever need anything or anyone to talk to, or if you just feel like hanging out, you know where to find me."

You back away from the door with your gun ready, in case he comes out of the room firing. You jog down the stairs, loud enough that you know he can hear you. Above you, the floor creaks. He's moving, but you're not sure if he's coming downstairs.

You look at the bags with regret. There was some good stuff in there, including more antibiotics. You think you know where they are, so you reach for that bag. You rummage through it as fast as you can. Finding it, you turn and come face to face with the boy. He's aiming his pistol directly at your chest.

"I thought you said you were leaving without taking anything."

Caught red-handed, you decide to tell the truth. "It's just some antibiotics. I've got some infected wounds. This is the only thing that will work." You hope the boy will have some compassion, but he doesn't say anything. "I'll trade you for them."

That seems to work. "Like what?"

"What would you like? Food? Pop? I'll tell you what. I have a twelve pack of Coke and two steaks that have to be eaten today, or they'll go bad. I'll cook one for you."

The boy is thinking. "Okay. Deal."

You smile. "Well, stop over in about an hour, and I'll fire up the grill."

"Cool."

You go home, unload your day's findings and dig out the steaks. You sniff them.

"Damn! I sure hope they're still good."

Andy shows up as the steaks are almost done. You've also made a couple of potatoes and set the table, and as he walks up the deck steps, you say, "Hi."

"Hi."

He stands there, unsure of what to do, looking uncomfortable.

"Inside the house on the counter, there are some drinks. Go grab whatever you like."

He comes back with a warm Coke.

"Dinner's ready." You put the steaks and spuds on two plates and bring them to the table. "Man, I hope they taste as good as they look."

Andy sits, his eyes wide at the size of his steak.

You laugh. "Yeah, they're big. Don't feel like you have to eat it all. You can take the leftovers home. They will last a few more days since they've been cooked."

Silence settles over the table as you both dig in. The meat is slightly chewy, but you barely notice. The taste is what counts, and you haven't had a meal so fine since before…you glance at the graves, then quickly away.

"Guess you liked it," you say, noticing Andy's plate is clean long before yours. Knowing you may not find more meat that will still be edible, you take your time and enjoy it. Andy obviously doesn't have the same mindset. He saw it, he ate it. Now he looks longingly at your plate.

"Did you even taste it?"

He nods. "Yeah. It was good." As an afterthought, he adds,

"Thanks."

"If you're still hungry, there are some packaged fruit pies. Go grab a couple."

He jumps up and almost runs inside. He comes back with two pies, an apple and a peach. You finish your steak as he is licking the sugar glaze from his fingers.

You push your plate away, satisfied, and lean back. Andy gets nervous under your scrutiny. Before he leaves you say, "So, what are your plans?"

"Plans?" He shrugs. "Like what?"

"That's what I'm asking you. What do you plan to do to survive?"

"I don't know."

"You do know that the world will never be the same, right?"

Another shrug. "I guess."

"Then you have to start thinking about staying alive. You know how to do that?"

Shrug. "Sure."

You nod. "That's good. But let me propose something to you. Let's work as a team. We can strip the houses of supplies and share them. If you want, you can move in here. That way, we can look out for each other. The area seems safe enough for now, but soon, it will be crawling with scavengers. They'll want what you have and will kill to get it. I've seen it happen already. If we stick together, we can watch each other's backs. What do you think?"

You frown as he gives you another shrug.

"Well, you know where to find me. Think about it."

He nods. "Okay."

You take the plates inside and give them a damp towel wipe. You don't want to waste water, but you don't want a bunch of dirty plates piling up, either. You go back outside to find Andy gone.

You smile and give a shrug of your own.

Chapter 3

You leave the house later than intended. Having stayed up late to put your collected items away, you overslept. You feel better about survival on a short-term basis, but don't want to leave it to chance. Having gone through more than a dozen houses now, you understand just how much work is ahead of you. You also know that time is an enemy. Food will rot and others will come.

Andy doesn't show up, but you're not surprised. Maybe he'll come around later, but if not, you're used to going it alone. You look for him as you drive to the first house.

Go to *** on page 133

Chapter 3

You leave the house later than intended. Having stayed up late to put your collected items away, you overslept. You feel better about survival on a short-term basis, but don't want to leave it to chance. Having gone through more than a dozen houses now, you understand just how much work is ahead of you. You also know that time is an enemy. Food will rot and others will come. You know of at least one person already working the area.

What happens if you run into him again? Will he be friendly, or try to eliminate his competition—you? You can't afford to take a chance. You have your gun ready and have practiced drawing it. You were slow. One of your goals today is to find a holster so you don't have to keep it loose at the back of your belt.

***

You drive the van to the house you where you stopped yesterday. Last night you rummaged through your drawers until you found the original plat map given to you when you built the house. You checked off the houses you already went through and set a goal of ten houses each day. Ambitious, but you think it's doable.

You go through the first five pretty quick. You are pleased to find two more guns: a .22 handgun with only a handful of bullets, and a shotgun four shells. Still, it is nice to have the extra firepower.

You take a break just after noon and have an apple, a granola bar, and a sports drink. Then you drive to the next street. You turn the corner, and at the end of the block you see a white van drive past on the cross street. You brake. Do you:

3A) follow? Page 134

3B) turn around and go home? Page 158

3A) You pull the gun from your belt and set it on the passenger seat as you drive to the end of the street. You look left. You don't see the van. Curious yet cautious, you make the turn, keeping your speed low. You glance up all the driveways you pass to make sure he hasn't pulled in somewhere or is lying in wait to spring an ambush.

You reach the next corner and look both ways. The side streets are shorter, but you don't see the van. It also is not ahead of you. You estimate the time it took you to get to the first corner and how fast the van was moving. If it had stayed on the road, you would've seen it. It had to have turned, but which way?

Left will bring you within a block of being back home. That thought gnaws at you. What if, while you were out collecting, your rival is emptying your house? Though it doesn't seem likely. you can't shake it. You turn left, drive to the end of the block and look left toward your house, midway down the street. No van or any other strange vehicle is parked in your driveway or on the street. You can recognize every car within five houses on either side of yours. The van is not here.

You turn around in a driveway and trace your route back the way you came. At the end of the next short street, you stop again. To the right is a court—a dead end. To the left, the road goes straight for two-thirds of the block before curving to the left and out of view.

You don't see the van to the right, but a thought strikes you: what if he's in a garage? That's what you'd do if you were at your home base. Unless you are willing to get out and check each house, you have no way to know for sure. You opt for the left turn.

Reaching the bend in the road, you stop. The road connects with the main one that runs through the entire subdivision. Still nothing. You move on. With each house you pass, your anxiety deepens. You feel like you're getting closer. All you need is suspenseful music to make it a scene from a movie; one where the bad guy jumps out and surprises the piss out of the hero.

A strange notion enters your mind. *Are you the hero or the fodder, put into the movie for the sole purpose of dying at the hands of the killer?* No. Not funny. You shake the thought from your mind.

Reaching the end of the street again, you check both ways. The road to the right leads out of the subdivision and to the main road toward town. The left will lead back toward home. You analyze why he would come this way. He was either leaving the area and didn't even live here, or he's in one of the houses you passed. He wouldn't come this way just to turn back the way he came. That makes no sense. If he was leaving the subdivision, he'd have stayed on the main road until he exited not make a detour along the back streets of the subdivision.

Then, a third possibility comes to you. What if all this was just to lure you out? Maybe it's an ambush. You look around nervously. If that's the case, wouldn't he have already attacked? Or was his plan to follow you home so he knows where you are?

Putting the van in park, you reach for the shotgun. You load the four shells and set it within reach. Scanning your mirrors, you don't see anyone coming up behind. Relieved but still unable to relax, you turn the van around and drive back the way you came.

As you reach the bend in the road, the white van is coming toward you. The driver brakes upon seeing you. The shocked expression on his face mirrors yours. It's apparent he was not setting a trap, because he's surprised to see you. Will he be friendly or try to kill you? You can't afford to make a mistake. Your life is on the line. Do you:

3A1) floor it and drive past? Page 136

3A2) hold your position? Page 142

3A3) reverse and run? Page 152

3A1) Not sure what to do, you keep your foot on the brake while reaching for the shotgun. Your eyes are locked on his, and when you see them narrow, you expect trouble.

You slide the shotgun onto your legs, barrel pointing at the door. The driver's side window lowers on the other van and you floor it. You pass him before he can do anything. You watch in the rearview mirror and see him lean out of the window holding a gun. He fires at you. You hear a bullet ping the van. Reaching the corner, you whip around it, the van threatening to topple. You right it, sideswipe a parked car, and keep going, but where should you go?

You don't want to lead him back to your house, so you need to lose him. You have a head start because he has to turn around, but your lead will not last long. You turn left at the next intersection, driving away from your house.

Searching in desperation, your eyes stop on a garage with the doors up. You have an idea. You swing the wheel and brake to slow. Hitting the driveway at high speed, the van bounces. You drive into the garage, throw it in park and jump out. You pull the cord to release the lock and lower the door manually. In your haste, it lands hard. Was it loud enough that your pursuer heard? You have to know.

You run to the opposite end of the garage and try the door to the house. It's locked. You curse and kick it once. Thinking fast, you pull out your wallet and grab a credit card. It's not like you'll ever need it again if it gets ruined. You insert it between the door and the frame and angle it toward the latch. You lean on the door, allowing the card to push the latch back. The door pops open and you run through the house.

At the front window, you inch the curtain aside and peer out. Nothing is moving out there. You either lost him, or he decided not to pursue. You watch for ten minutes, and then the van comes to the curb right in front of you and idles.

A chill dances up your spine. The driver seems to be giving the house an extra-long look. Did he remember the garage door had been up? But, why? The van shifts like someone inside is moving. You reach for your gun and feel the panic grip your heart when you discover it's gone. Then you remember you'd put it on the seat.

With a last look at the van, you run to the garage and retrieve the handgun. You slide it in your belt at the front of your pants and pick up the shotgun. Reentering the house, you turn toward the front room and freeze as a shadow passes the window, heading toward the side of the house.

Though you can 't see him, you make a guess where he is. You realize with a start that if he's going around to the back of the house, you'll be in full view from the patio door. You quick step into the front room, then go through the dining room and enter the kitchen from the opposite side. You duck behind the kitchen cabinets.

Crouching, you peer around the corner and see a man's face pressed against the glass. His eyes scan your way and you pull back. Did he see you? You hold your breath, afraid he can hear you breathing. You exhale in a burst as you hear him try the door, which is locked. You want to look again, needing to know where he is, yet afraid of being discovered. Instead, you sit against the cabinet and wait. A minute later, you hear a noise coming from the dining room.

You crawl to the doorway, lie down and peer out. The man is looking through the window. He must be standing on something, because his head is well above the sill. You have a desire to run, but how far could you get before he came after you again? Best to finish it here.

He turns in your direction, but this time, you pull back too late. The expression on his face makes it obvious he's spotted you. What do you do now? You decide to spin around in the doorway and fire the shotgun through the window, but before you can, something crashes through the glass patio door.

You turn that direction, not sure if the man has smashed through or tossed something. Either way, you have a breach. You level the shotgun and wait. Long, nerve-racking minutes pass with no movement. You are anxious to make a move, but you wonder if he is waiting on the other side of the cabinets.

A second crash comes from the dining room behind you. The first crash was a diversion. You whirl around to confront him, stepping through the doorway. There is no way you can miss him with the shotgun. Still, nothing moves. You step closer, heart racing like a meteor. Nothing. Closer. Nothing. Then, you see a large rock on the floor and realize you were mistaken.

To your shock, you realize this was the diversion. You spin just as the first bullets hail. Your arm is on fire, but you ignore it. To shift your focus is to die. The man is in the doorway firing a handgun. *Keep moving*! your mind screams. You fall to the side, hoping to use the dining room table for cover, if you're still alive when you reach the floor.

Though not on target, you press the trigger. The shotgun roars in the small room. It kicks upward as you land on your shoulder. The barrel cracks you on the forehead. A bullet follows you. The man is now crouching below the table, trying to get a bead on you from between the table and chair legs.

You roll as he fires again. The bullet grazes your head. You are stunned to see the man rise and walk around the table. You position the shotgun and pull the trigger as he appears above you. His gun barks once before your shot obliterates his face. His body is thrown backward into the wall.

You lay there, frozen and in shock. Once the adrenaline bleeds off, you try to sit up, but a sharp pain in your side stops you. You touch the spot and your hand comes away bloody. *Damn!* He hit you. You think of the woman that died and pray the bullet went all the way through.

Using the shotgun for leverage, you push up to a sitting position. The pain is steady now. You gasp from the effort. Reaching behind you, you feel for an exit wound and to your relief, you find one. You gather your strength and get to your feet. On your way through the kitchen, you snag a dish towel and press it against the entry hole. Your hand stretches wide enough to cover both holes, but it doesn't do much good. You hurry upstairs and go through the medicine cabinet, finding gauze pads and tape. Doubling up the pads, you tape them in place. The blood soaks through. You need something tighter.

You rip the sheet off the bed and begin cutting it in long strips as you did before. You reach for more gauze pads, then change your mind. Under the sink you find a box of maxi pads. You press one on each side of the wound and wrap the strips over the top. You use the whole sheet, winding each strip around yourself twice. You pull them tight and tie the ends in front of you.

You need to get home and lie down. You already feel weak from the blood loss. You wipe sweat from your forehead with the back of your hand, only to find it, too, is bleeding. You remember the searing heat where a bullet grazed you. Then you touch your arm and remember you were also hit there. You are a mess.

You put gauze pads over each wound and tape them in place. At this rate, your injuries will never fully heal. You go down to the van, leaving everything the way it is. You lift the garage door, which sends a blast of pain through your body, and drive home in a daze.

The wounds need to be cleaned, but you're too exhausted. You lie down on the sofa, and although you keep prodding yourself to get up, in minutes you're asleep.

Chapter 4

A noise wakes you. You open your eyes, but they take a moment to focus. You feel feverish. If you are going to have any chance to survive, you need to take care of your wounds. You rise on shaky legs and stagger into the kitchen. Your medical supplies are right there on the counter. You've used them so many times in the past few days they've becomes staples.

You clean each one with soap and water, then flush them with a liberal amount of peroxide that makes you scream. Blotting them dry, you smear triple antibiotic cream over each and dress them. A major benefit of searching the homes has been the discovery of a multitude of antibiotic pills. They are a mix of prescriptions, none of which mean anything to you, but as before, something is better than nothing.

Without having internet access, a trip to the library for a medical journal will be necessary. Until then, you swallow two from the fullest pill bottle and hope for the best.

Grabbing two bottles of water, you go back to the couch. Downing one bottle, you lay back and close your eyes. You hear the noise again and remember why you woke in the first place. Someone else is in the house.

In an instant, your mind clears and all pain is pushed aside as you try to think where you placed the guns. You were so out of it when you got home, you don't remember, but they aren't near you. You try to recall if you locked the doors, but again, the memory is unclear.

Damn!

Rolling to the floor as soundlessly as you can, you crawl toward the kitchen. You lean forward and peek. A woman is standing with her back to you. She tilts her head back as she drinks a bottle of water. One of *your* waters.

Getting a foot beneath you, you rise to a crouching position. The woman stiffens, as if sensing something. She turns and you rush her. She screams, and when you see the gun in her hand, so do you.

She shakes her head with terror in her eyes and says, "No."

You hit her across the chest with your arm and drive her into the counter. She is bent at the waist and as she falls, her head strikes the counter with a resounding *thud*. She moans and collapses as you rip the gun from her hand.

Once you catch your breath and the adrenaline stops spiking, you drag her into the family room and lay her on the couch. You sit in the easy chair across from her. Was she working with the man you killed? Seems likely, but she had the chance to kill you when you were asleep. Maybe she didn't know you were there. She knew where you live, though.

As you watch her, you decide to give her a chance to explain, but trust will not come easy, especially since she had a gun in her hand.

Continue Chapter 4 at * * * on Page 173

3A2) You reach for the shotgun. If he comes for you, you're prepared. Neither of you move, though. It's like a game of chicken. Whoever moves first will lose. You don't intend to lose, but if he doesn't do something soon, you're gonna leave.

Another two minutes pass, then he drives forward and angles across the road, blocking you. You shift into reverse. The passenger window slides down and the man leans across the seat. Almost too late, you see the gun. It barks three times as you duck below the dash. You see the three holes in the windshield. Your heart thumps wildly.

Without looking at the road, you press the accelerator and the van shoots backward. You lift your head high enough to glimpse the van. Flashes tell you he's shooting again. You can't see where you're going, but you know the road curves. You'll have to turn soon, or you'll crash. Then, it happens. You hit a parked car.

The impact throws you forward and almost off the seat. The shotgun falls to the floor. You sit up to see the van turn and approach you. You only have a few seconds to decide what to do. Do you:

3A2a) keep driving blindly backward? Page 143

3A2b) get out? Page 144

3A2c) put the van in drive? Page 149

3A2a) You push harder on the pedal, but the van does not move. It is lodged against the parked vehicle. You swing the wheel side to side to break free, but that doesn't work, either. The white van is once again blocking your path.

You shift into drive, but with no room to maneuver, your only choice is to ram the other van. You sit up, floor the accelerator and watch the collision. You yank the shift into reverse, turn the wheel hard and race backward until you ram the car behind you. Again, you turn the wheel hard and shift into drive. There is another crash, but this time closer to the cab end. One more hit and you should be free. You shift into reverse and scan for the other man. To your surprise, he is not in the driver's seat. You glance around. *Did he get out of the van?*

You shoot backward. As you shift for your final forward push, a shadow appears at your window. You look and see an angry face glaring at you, but what sends fear through your soul is the barrel of his gun pressed against the glass. You mash the pedal down and duck, knowing both actions will be too late to save you.

The window shatters, and one after another, bullets pound into your vehicle. When the vans collide this time, you are unaware. A hand reaches through the window and shuts off the engine. The door opens and you tumble out. You don't feel the impact with the street.

Your last sight is of the angry man stepping over you, climbing into your van. He scans the items—your items--and smiles down at you. Then he's gone, along with everything else.

End

3A2b) You open the door and jump out, then reach back in and grab the shotgun. The other van screeches to a stop in the middle of the road. You run to the rear of the other van and duck below the back windows. You wait. He will be searching for you. If he comes out either front door or the sliding door, you'll have the advantage. His best bet is to drive away. Or—*shit!* The van revs and you dive to the side as it lurches backward.

You roll, get to your feet and run toward the driver's window. Your eyes meet in the side mirror. You see panic in his. He shifts into drive as you get close to the door. The van shoots forward and you unload your bullets into the door. You keep running and firing until all four shells are gone.

You stop then, realizing you have no other gun. It's still on the front seat. You're about to go back to get it, when you see the van jump the curb, cross over a front lawn and crash into a house. Do you:

3A2b1) go after it? Page 145

3A2b2) go back to the van and leave? Page 146

3A2b3) go back to the van and retrieve your gun? Page 147

3A2b1) You run after the van. Reaching it, you go around and creep along the passenger side. You can't see the driver in the mirror. He is either too injured to sit up or he's ducking down, waiting. You peek through the window and find him slouched against the driver's window, covered in blood. You reach through the window and unlock the door. Easing it open, your eyes never leaving him, you step up and lean across the seat for the key.

You shut off the engine. The driver isn't moving, and you can't tell if he's breathing. You watch for a moment, then allow your gaze to drift toward the cargo section. Like yours, it's full of useful things. You smile. Then you look back at the man and your smile fades. One eye is open and looking at you. By some miracle, he is still alive. You stare at him for a few seconds, then you are chilled by the bloody smile stretching across his face. You are puzzled until you notice the gun in his hand. He pulls the trigger as you try to back out. The bullet bores through your forehead and out the back of your skull.

Should've gone back for your gun.

End

3A2b2) You go back to the van and debate with yourself. The safe approach wins. You get in the van, work the wheel to be clear of the mess and drive away. You begin to tremble at dodging another life-threatening situation.

You get home, park in the garage and close the overhead door. You busy yourself with unloading the van to keep from thinking about how close you came to death—again. You must be more careful. You need to make better and smarter decisions. And for damn sure, you have to understand this is a different world. You can't trust anyone.

You go inside, open one of the warm beers you just collected and sit down.

Chapter 4 go to Page 139

3A2b3) You run back to your van and climb inside. You search for your Sig Sauer and find it under the passenger seat. You approach the other van quickly, watching the mirrors and the reverse lights. You don't see the driver. You peek in the passenger side window. The driver is a bloody heap leaning against the shattered driver's side window. He's not moving, and you can't tell from there if he's breathing.

You reach through the window and unlock the door. Keeping your gun trained on him, you ease the door open. The man does not move. You step up and lean inside. The van is full of the same types of items you're collecting. You reach over and shut the engine off.

You prod him with the barrel of the gun. He doesn't stir. Keeping the barrel against his body, you take a better look at the interior of the van. You feel your gun move, and you jump back as the man raises his gun toward you. You panic, scream, and pull the trigger repeatedly. You have no idea how many times you fire, but there's no longer any doubt whether he's alive.

You step out of the van and fight back the urge to vomit. As your breathing and heart rate slow, you walk around to the driver's side, open the door, and let the body fall out. The man's fingers are still wrapped around the gun. You wrench it from his dead grip and toss it inside the van.

After a few more minutes to recover from the shock, you go back to your van and drive home. You pull into the garage, then walk back to get the other van.

You spend the rest of the day unloading. It's late by the time you're done. You make a quick meal and lie down on the couch in the family room. Your last thought before falling asleep is that you're gonna need a new van.

Chapter 4

A noise wakes you. You open your eyes, but they take a moment to focus. With a jolt of panic, you realize someone else is in the house.

In an instant, your mind clears and all pain is pushed aside as you think about where you placed the guns. You were so out of it when you got home, you don't remember, but they aren't with you. You try to recall if you locked the doors, but again, the memory is unclear.

Damn!

Rolling to the floor as soundlessly as you can, you crawl toward the kitchen. You lean forward and peek in. A woman is standing with her back to you. She tilts her head back, drinking a bottle of water. One of *your* waters.

Getting a foot beneath you, you rise to a crouching position. The woman stiffens, as if alerted to something. She turns and you rush her. She screams, and when you see the gun in her hand, so do you.

She shakes her head with terror in her eyes and says, "No."

You hit her across the chest with your arm drive her into the counter, bent at the waist. As she falls, her head strikes the counter with a resounding *thud*. She moans and collapses as you rip the gun from her hand.

Once you catch your breath and the adrenaline stops spiking, you drag her into the family room and lay her on the couch. You sit in the easy chair across from her. Was she working with the man you killed? Seems likely, but she had the chance to kill you when you were asleep. Maybe she didn't know you were there. She knew where you live, though.

As you watch her, you decide to give her a chance to explain, but she will have to earn your trust, especially since she had a gun in her hand.

Continue Chapter 4 at * * * on Page 173

3A2c) You shift into drive as you see the other van start toward you. It swings in front of you, but you shove the pedal down and spin the wheel hard to the left. You ram the rear of the van and push it to the side. The air bag explodes in your face, stunning you. You're dazed, but as your mind clears, you realize you are still moving.

You go up a driveway on an angle. You spin the wheel and shoot across the front lawn. A shot whizzes by. You duck as it pierces the side panel. You aim the van toward the street and see a man running toward you, gun up, from the corner of your eye.

The van bounces onto the street. You swing the wheel, fighting for control. The man is large in the passenger side mirror. If he is even with you, he'll have an easy shot. You slam on the brakes and skid to a stop. The man is slower to stop his momentum and is now in front of you. You slam your foot down, but the van is slow to accelerate.

The man raises his gun and you duck as a bullet bores through the windshield. He runs to the side to avoid being hit, but you stay on him. The van makes contact but is not fast enough to do much damage. He dives to the side and you lose track of him. You keep going, and in the mirror, you see him line up aim a shot, then think better of it. He runs for his van.

That gives you an idea and the opening you need. You park and get out. You pick the shotgun up off the floor, hit the unlock button, and run around to the passenger side. You find the handgun under the seat and put it in your belt in the front of your pants.

You step away from van and aim the shotgun. The other van is approaching and has enough distance to accelerate. Holding the shotgun steady, you fire once. The windshield spider webs twice. More damage. The van gets closer. The man's head is a small curve above the dash. Three. Directly into the radiator. Steam erupts.

You don't have time for a fourth. You dive in front of your van as your opponent drives past. You have already decided to let him flee if he keeps driving. You will not pursue, but if he stops, you're gonna end this.

You jump to your feet and run after the van. It goes a little farther down the road, but then coughs a few times. The speed fades and eventually the van comes to a stop.

After a few more running steps to get a shooting angle, you stop as well. If he exits, he's dead. You wait, but he doesn't emerge. The van rocks, though, and you think he's going for the passenger door.

Crouching, you run to the driver's rear quarter panel. You can feel the van moving as the man positions for whatever he's planning. The sliding door on the other side opens. You drop to the ground and aim underneath the van. The man jumps to the ground and you pull the trigger.

He shouts in pain, but you don't wait to see what happens. You leave the now-empty shotgun and pull the handgun as you get to your feet. You run toward the front of the van as a bullet ricochets under it. Not wanting to take a bullet in the foot, you stop at the front tire for protection.

Now what?

You hear a voice.

"Hey man! I give up. Don't shoot."

You think for a moment. *Should you trust him after he tried to kill you?* No, but it doesn't mean you need to be cold-blooded and kill him.

"Throw your gun out so I can see it and roll away from the van."

"Man, I'm trusting you. I'm hurt. Bad. I can't defend myself, so please. I'm begging you. Don't shoot."

"Toss the gun out, or I'll have to."

A few seconds later, a handgun bounces off the street and skitters towards you. Keeping your feet behind the wheel, you bend over and peer upside down at the man. If anything, he looks like he's pressed in closer to the van.

"Okay, I tossed the gun out. Now, don't shoot."

You decide to test him. "Did you roll away from the van?"

"Yeah, a little, but I can't walk. You shot both of my legs. I'm bleeding bad."

"Okay. I'm coming. I've got some medical supplies. I'll help you."

You kneel behind the tire and bend down to look under the van. You see he is holding a gun pointed toward the front of the van. It's a trap.

He calls out. "Are you coming? I need help. Hurry."

"Yeah," you say under the van, "I don't think so."

He locks eyes with you. He rolls and tries to bring the gun on target, but you fire first, three times. His body jerks with the impacts. You run around the front of the van and aim at him. He is writhing, the gun on the cement near his head.

You run forward and kick it away.

He looks up at you. His face is contorted with agony. He speaks. It sounds like "Bastard," but it's hard to tell with his mouth full of blood. His body twitches a few times, then stops.

You stare at him long after he expires. You don't feel nearly as bad about killing him as you thought you might. Guess it makes a difference when someone is also trying to kill you. *Why do people feel they must kill? There can't be that many of us left. We should all be able to work together for our survival.* It just doesn't make sense to you.

You pick up both of his guns and drive home. After emptying your van, you take several trips back and forth between his van and your house, grabbing his take. Darkness has long fallen by the time you finish.

Too exhausted to climb the stairs, you fall asleep on the couch in the family room.

Go to Chapter 4 Page 139

3A3) You slam the shift into reverse and turn the wheel hard. The tires ram up the curb. As you shift, you see the van coming at you. You press the pedal down and lurch forward. No sooner did you straighten the van on the street than you are hit from behind. You fishtail, but as you accelerate, you get control.

You reach the corner and turn left. You assume your vehicle is evenly matched with his, and you will not be able to outrun him. Still, you gun the engine, if only to get some distance ahead and time to think. You only manage about ten feet of clearance before the gap is closed. He rams you again.

In seconds, you reach the back end of the subdivision and must decide which way to turn. In your mind, it's the same distance either way, but you choose right because it leads to many open country roads. As you make the turn, the chase van smacks your rear quarter panel, sending you sideways. It was a smart move, you think.

He continues his maneuver until you are side by side but facing opposite directions. Maybe it wasn't so smart. He raises his hand and you spot the gun. Pushing the pedal down hard, you duck instinctively as a bullet shatters the passenger window. It misses, but you get a few cuts from flying shards.

You break contact and are now moving away from him. Ahead, the road curves to the left. You accelerate and gain some distance. You are midway down the long block when the van comes around the bend. Do you:

3A3a) stop and confront him? Page 153

3A3b) try to outrun him? Page 156

3A3a) With some distance to work with, you decide to make a stand. You stop even with a parked car and get out. You grab the two guns and stand in front of the parked car. The other van bears down on you as if it's going to ram, but at the last minute, the driver brakes.

He stares at you but doesn't move. You're not an expert with guns, but you think the distance is too great for a shotgun to be effective. The standoff continues, making you antsy. You wish he'd do something. The longer you stand there, the more nervous you get.

Should you make a move? What? Do you charge him, guns blazing, or get back in the van and drive off? How would he react to either of those? Would he back away if you charged him, or stick a gun out the window, now that you're out in the open? And if you drove away, wouldn't he just follow again?

No, you can't drive away. This has to end here and now.

The other man must have come to the same conclusion. He shifts into reverse. Now is your chance.

You leave the shelter of the parked car and run at the van. He doesn't notice you at first, but when he's backed up far enough to turn around safely, he sees you and pauses. Now the choice is his--to stand and fight or drive off.

You close the gap in a hurry. You need to be as close as possible for the shotgun to have any chance to hit the target. You are almost within what you consider to be range, when the van shoots forward. He could just run you down. You hadn't thought about that.

Standing in the middle of the street with no cover, you have limited options. You are too far away to run for the van. You can't dive to the side until he is much closer, or he will just adjust his path and use you as a speed bump. The only other choice is to hold your ground and shoot.

You aim the shotgun and see his body slump low, not giving you much to shoot at, but you do have other targets. You fire one at the windshield, pock-marking the glass, before lowering your aim to the radiator. You shoot the second shell and it hisses, but the speed still increases. You step to the side to get a better angle at the tires and fire your gun, but the driver adjusts and is bearing down on you.

You fake a dive to the left, and as he corrects to follow, you dive to the right. He is too slow to adjust and passes you.

You jump up and follow. He brakes for an instant, but sees you in the side mirror and gives it gas again. Still, that one second of slowing brings you close. As he tries to go around the van, he hits the curb and bounces upward. The slight slowing is enough to bring you alongside of the driver's door, and you don't hesitate. The shotgun erupts. The window shatters and the man screams. A bloody mist fills the air. You know you've scored a hit, but you don't know how bad it is.

You drop the shotgun and yank the handgun free. A round was previously chambered, so you cock it and fire. The bullet goes through the window, but hits the windshield. A bloody hand holding a gun emerges from the window. You are close enough to reach it. You slap it aside as it fires and the bullet ricochets off the street with a whine.

The van is still moving, but not fast. You jump on the running board and jamming your gun inside the van, pulling the trigger three times as fast as you can. The van strikes a small tree in front of a house and stops. You look inside and see the man is no longer moving. In fact, the side of his head has a large hole in it.

You reach in and shut off the engine, then step down, opening the door to let the body fall out.

This didn't have to happen. If only he wanted to talk and work together, he'd still be alive and you'd have an ally. It didn't make sense that people should survive the apocalypse, only to kill each other off. This world is crazier than the former.

You drive home and park your van, then hike back for the other one. It limps up your driveway and stalls out, which is somehow fitting.

You spend the rest of the day and early evening unloading the haul. Then, after a quick meal you go to sleep on the couch in the family room, hoping the next day will be less exciting.

Go to Chapter 4 Page 139

3A3b) You drive hard until the road dead ends into the main east-west road. Town is to the right. You opt for the left, toward more rural roads and likely less trouble.

You make the turn and still have a lead, but the pursuing van takes the turn at high speed. For a moment, you think—even hope—the van will tip over, but the driver rights the vehicle and is soon closing the gap.

Shit!

Outrunning him is not going to happen. You increase your speed, but the other vehicle has more horsepower. The gap narrows. You need a plan.

You reach over to the passenger seat and collect your guns. A look in the side mirror shows your opponent in the other lane, attempting to come up alongside. You can't allow that. You cut him off and force him to slow and get behind you.

Over the next few miles, he tries several more times, but you hold him off. You swerve back and forth to prevent him from passing. It slows you down, but he can't get at you.

Then he revs up and rams your bumper. The jolt snaps your head back into the headrest. He rams again, this time from the side, sending the van fishtailing. You gain control, but this has to end. If he wants to play like that, you'll oblige him.

Angry and not really thinking it through, you wait until he makes his next run at you and slam on your brakes. He smashes into you, breaking glass, rending metal, and screeching tires. Your vehicle swerves, and it is only by luck you don't flip.

You keep your foot on the brake and slam the stick into park. The transmission grinds and you fear you've trashed it, but no matter; you fling the door open and jump out with a gun in each hand.

He has a similar idea, but he's a step behind, taken by surprise with your sudden braking. You level the shotgun as he steps down and unload all four shells into him. His bloody pulp of a body sags to the ground, leaving red streaks down the van.

It didn't have to be this way. He chose the play, but you ended the game. Can you trust anyone?

You turn from the mess and walk back to your van. As you feared, the transmission is locked up. You sigh. It will be a long day.

You get in the other van and drive it home. By the time you make several trips to unload, the sun has long set. You make a quick meal and go to sleep on the couch in the family room, praying for a lot less excitement the following day.

Go to Chapter 4 Page 139

3B) Not sure you're ready for a confrontation, you go home. There's still a lot of daylight left, but if the other guy is out looting houses, there's good chance you'll run into each other. You need to think things through before that happens. You'd much rather talk to him than fight, but that will be up to him, not you. You want to make sure that you're the last man standing.

At your driveway, you open the garage and pull in, then get out to close the overhead door behind you. As you do, you see the white van stop at the corner. Your heart leaps to your throat. You shut the door fast and it slams against the cement. You flick the lock in place and grab the guns from the front seat.

You run into the house and watch from the front window. The van is still there. You set the handgun down and load the shotgun.

As you watch, you ponder the possibilities. Will he come as friend or foe? If a friend, how much do you trust him? If a foe, how close do you let him get to you? Too many variables; too many outcomes.

The van edges into the turn and stops broadside to the house. You have no doubt he has seen you. He knows you are here, watching him. He drives past, turning at the next intersection and disappears.

Now what?

You wait, but he doesn't return. You relax a bit, but you know he'll be back. Thirty minutes later, you still haven't seen him. Do you:

3B1) unload the van? Page 159

3B2) keep your vigil? Page 167

3B3) go upstairs to get a better view? Page 169

3B1) You decide to unload the van. With so much to carry, the shotgun proves to be a hindrance, so you set it down on the workbench in the garage. If anyone comes, you'll hear them in advance and still have the handgun.

You haul everything downstairs and begin to sort your new stock. You're excited by a find of canned beef stew, one of your favorites as a boy. You set a can aside for dinner. Your mouth waters.

Halfway through your work, you hear the floor creak above you. You freeze. It has to be your imagination. You didn't hear glass breaking or wood splintering. You listen for what feels like an hour, and you don't hear anything else. You go back to stocking, but you slow your pace and work as quietly as possible.

After another few minutes of silence, you figure the noise was just the house settling; nothing out of the ordinary. Then, another creak, but this time near the basement door, and there is no denying the source: a footfall. Someone is in the house.

You set down the cans you are holding and withdraw your gun. Moving to a position where you have some cover and still see the stairs, you crouch, wait and watch. You know you left the door open. Whoever is up there is most likely doing the same thing you are. You decide to make your presence known.

You drag the full bag of cans across the floor. The noise echoes. Holding the gun in your right hand, you reach into the bag with your left and extract one can after another, setting each one on a metal shelf. The cans smack and scrape, hopefully making just enough noise to make the intruder believe it is safe to venture down.

With the bag now empty and still no sign of anyone, you start humming. You pick up the cans and set them back down on the shelf again to keep making noise. The humming morphs into singing. The song came out of nowhere, and after you begin singing, you realize you don't know all the words, so you make them up as you go.

Your throat catches when you see the foot land on the step. Someone is descending and you doubt it's because he's a fan of your singing and wants an autograph. He has taken the bait and the stealthy approach tells you all you need to know about his purpose.

You are so focused on the invader that you drop a can. "Shit!" It comes out in a natural flow. Another step down. You can see his jeans up to the knee. You take a steady aim, placing your arm across the shelf, and continue singing. You only have the space between two stairs for a target, but at this distance you feel confident you'll hit him.

He stops and stoops to take a look. You remember you need to cock your gun for the first shot. You look from the gun to the steps. His torso appears and there isn't much time. You cough to cover the sound of the hammer being pulled. The intruder pauses.

You go back to singing and reach for another can. A line of tension stretches between you and the intruder. Sweat trickles from your forehead into the corner of your eye and burns. You cannot afford to blink or wipe it away. You stay focused on the target, your finger tightening around the trigger.

Then, you see the legs straighten. In a rush, without thought, you race from your hiding place, bumping into the shelf and knocking cans to the floor. You hear running above you and hurry to the stairs. Disregarding caution, you take the stairs two at a time, only stopping when you reach the door.

The figure is at the patio door frantically working the lock. As the door swings open, you freeze. It's a woman. Her face registers fear. She bolts out before you can speak the word "Wait!"

You follow, but stop when you hear the scream; one that sounds prematurely cut off.

Slowing your pursuit and curious, you advance toward the patio door, gun raised and on alert. Before you can get there, the figure comes back, but not by her own will. Behind her, a man has a gun to her head and an arm wrapped around her neck, holding her close to him. It is the man from the van.

You raise your gun up to a point above her shoulder. He ducks, only an eye and part of his forehead visible. You don't feel comfortable taking the shot, and you try not to let your hand tremble. You move behind the kitchen cabinets for cover.

The man pushes the woman inside the house. They are ten feet away from you. She is crying and afraid; his look and demeanor are more sinister. What's the play here? Is her fear real or an act? Are they working as a team to rob and maybe kill you?

Your nature is to protect women and children, but if she's playing you, you will shoot her.

"Put the gun down, or I'll shoot your woman."

"Shoot her. She's not my woman."

A flicker of confusion crosses the man's face. Then the sneer returns. "Yeah, right. Then why's she coming from your house?"

"The same reason you are, I would guess. To rob me."

"Oh, so you're all right with me shooting her, then?"

"No problem."

He sniffs her hair. "Or me having my way with her?"

"Take her. Just do it elsewhere."

She whimpers. It's convincing.

He looks uncertain now, and he decides to test you. He lowers his hand across her chest, pausing on a breast. He watches for your reaction.

You fight back the urge to shoot as you work hard to keep your expression free of emotion.

"This doesn't bother you, huh?"

"Not as much as it bothers her."

"Then she's mine."

"Take her."

She whimpers again. "No. Please."

If she's acting, she's good. There's real emotion in her voice.

"You two are working together anyway. So, before I shoot her and then I shoot you, get out."

Now he looks angry. This hasn't gone as he had planned. You get the feeling something's about to happen. You stoop below the cabinets, keeping your head and gun above. If he shoots her, you'll kill him. If he tries to shoot you, you'll be a more difficult target.

You're in a stalemate. Your mind whirls, searching for solutions. Do you:

3B1a) wait for him to make a move? Page 163

3B1b) try to shoot him? Page 165

3B1c) shoot through her, hoping to hit him? Page 166

3B1a) The tension builds as you stare at each other. You know he's trying to find a way to get you to flinch, if only for a second, and take the gun off him. All you want is for him to leave your house. He stops pawing at the woman as he thinks. She is crying silently. Again, you marvel at her acting skills.

"I'll give you the woman back if you give me half of your food supplies."

"No."

"Half. I know you been gathering stuff from the neighborhood. I've seen the stripped houses. Half isn't bad. You'll still have enough —and you get your ladyfriend back."

He sounds like he's begging.

"No."

A look of frustration flashes across his face, then his eyes narrow in an angry glare. You can tell he is getting ready to act. You force yourself to be calm, but you're anxious. Your finger tightens on the trigger.

In a sudden rush, he pushes the woman toward you. His gun hand moves from her head and swings in your direction as he shoves her to the other side of the cabinets. You duck left as he fires and crawl to the right. He'll have to lean over the countertop to get a look at you. You reach the end, lie on your stomach on the floor and peer around the side. You can see four legs. The woman's body blocks him from seeing you. You sight on one of the bigger legs, hoping you've guessed right, and pull the trigger.

Bone snaps, blood sprays, and a scream fills the house. One body drops and another falls toward the kitchen table. As his face comes into view four feet from you, you fire again, placing a neat round hole in his forehead.

The woman is screaming in a pitch that hurts your ears. She moves toward the door and you get to your feet.

"Stop!" You command, your gun focused on her back.

Her legs pump up and down like a child having a tantrum. She wails and sobs. "Please. Please. Please."

You take the gun off her and lift your arms to show you aren't a threat to her. She collapses in a heap, but then she jumps up and backs into the table as she sees the body sprawled close to her. She is in a panic and looks to be on the verge of a breakdown.

You step forward and she doesn't appear to notice. Her scream is one long continuous siren, only pausing for a quick intake of air. You step over the body and move closer. Now she sees you and pleads with you again.

"Please. Please. Please."

"Hey. Hey." She doesn't hear you. "Listen to me!" you shout and grab her arms. Your touch sends her into another frenzy. You shake her. "Stop and listen." Her eyes roll back and she collapses in your arms. You grab her to keep her from hitting the floor. Her dead weight is heavy as you try to lift her. You drag her into the family room and get her to the sofa.

You stare down at her. She looks so frail, so out of place in this new chaotic world. You wonder what she did before; you guess she was probably a teacher. You leave her and go back to the kitchen. Grabbing the man's feet, you drag him outside and down the deck steps, across the lawn, past the graves and a good hundred yards behind your property.

You drop him. "Asshole" is the only prayer you offer over his body. You start toward the house, then think better of it and go back. You search his pockets and find a second magazine for the gun and what you hoped to find—the van keys.

"Now your shit's mine."

You walk back to the house, wondering what strange direction this new world will take you next.

Go to Chapter 4 Page 173

3B1b) You struggle over what to do. If you wait much longer, you may not live to regret not acting when you had a chance. You should shoot, but you're afraid you'll miss and either hit the woman, or give your opponent an opening to shoot you.

You debate back and forth, wondering if the woman is working with him or is an innocent victim.

You're sweating again and fear it will burn and blur your vision as before. You won't have a chance if that happens. He'll see you blinking and take advantage of the situation. You can almost feel the bullet ripping through you.

You make up your mind right then; you aim and pull the trigger. The blast is much louder in the house and all three of you flinch. A second gunshot follows an instant later and the woman falls to the floor. The shock freezes you for a moment before an anger more powerful than any emotion you have ever felt grabs at your sanity. You fire the gun until the slide locks back.

As the smoke and odor waft away, you see the bloody heap of what had once been a human lying on the floor. You look from him to the woman as the adrenaline ebbs away. It leaves you exhausted. You want—no, *need* to sit down, but as you reach for the chair, you use it to steady your balance. Sucking in long, deep breaths, you clear your mind and set about the chore of removing the bodies.

You drag the man through the backyard and a long way from the house. You leave him there after removing the keys and spare mag from his pockets. You go back for the woman. You will always wonder if she was part of plan or not. You choose to believe that she was so you can cope with causing her death. It's a cold way to look at it, but your survival depended upon it.

You set her down next to the other woman's grave and go get the shovel. As you dig, you wonder how many others will find their final resting place to be your backyard.

Go to Chapter 4 Page 177

3B1c) The standoff can't go on for much longer. Sooner or later, one of you is going to make a mistake. You have to make sure it's not you. You have no shot at him, but you can shoot her. The bullet may or may not pass through her and hit him. You don't know enough about guns or bullets to make that determination, but it will eliminate her as a potential threat and remove his shield.

You switch aim to the woman, which takes them both by surprise. You hesitate, unable to shoot her. The man has a puckered 'Oh shit!' look and backs away from her, perhaps envisioning the bullet ripping through her and into himself.

You notice a wet spot appear at the woman's crotch and spread down both legs. She is terrified. She faints and hits the ground before her urine puddles there. Time seems to stand still as you are face to face with the man. Movement resumes, but in slow motion. Your gun is in a better shooting position than his. The gun bucks in your hand. You blink with the concussion. You fire again, trying to dodge to the side.

His gun fires and a flash lights your vision. Heat touches the side of your face. You blink again and shoot. His body arcs backward as he triggers another round. You fire quick successive shots and the man is blown back through the open door.

As movement returns to normal speed, you hear screaming and to your surprise, discover it's you. You close your mouth and the echo of gunshots surround you, distorting your senses.

It takes a long time before you feel like you can move without falling. You bend over the woman and feel a pulse. You try to pick her up, but don't have the strength. Dragging her to the family room, you manage to get her onto the couch.

You drag the man for a long distance behind your house. You search him and find a spare magazine and the van keys. It's already been a long day, and you need a nap, but with so much left to do, that's not going to happen.

You trudge back to the house and wonder what strange thing will happen next.

Go to Chapter 4 Page 173

3B2) You continue watching, sure the man will return. You move the sofa over so you can lean against it. You grow weary. Surveillance is perhaps the single most boring thing you've done since the world-ending event occurred.

A crash at the back of the house snaps you alert. Heavy footsteps are coming closer. You spin toward them and see a man burst into the room with gun in hand. You fire simultaneously, both shots missing. You take your next flurry of shots while retreating, and neither of you score a hit.

You can hear his raspy breathing, which means he can probably hear yours. You crouch next to the stairs and peer through the spindles. You don't see him, but catch movement in front of you. No one's there. Then you realize it is his reflection in the mirror hanging on the wall.

He is pressed against the wall in the foyer. He takes a nervous look over his shoulder, worried about you coming up behind him. You stand and move along the stairs and slide your gun hand through the spindles, aiming along the wall, while keeping watch in the mirror. If he pokes his head out even a little, you'll know in advance.

To your dismay, he turns and moves toward the kitchen. You are losing him. He stops and peers around the wall, looking into the kitchen. If he moves that way, you'll lose sight of him.

You wait. He peeks again, then comes back toward you. He crouches and edges closer to the corner. You have a good view of him. You adjust your aim down a bit and urge him to poke his head out. He does, but it is too quick to fire at. It was a test. You're sure he'll look again, longer this time, but he doesn't. He's looking at the bottom of the stairs and hasn't seen you. You have ample cover and feel confident with your position. It's the shot that has you concerned. You haven't fired a gun often enough to have developed any skill. The shot you intend to make is not an easy one. You will have to be quick, and you only have a small target to aim for.

You see him lower his body to the floor, only his legs still reflected in the mirror. From where you are, you won't be able to see when he crawls out. The stairs are blocking your angle; you have no shot. You watch as his legs move, the mirror displaying only his feet now, and know he is crawling to the opposite side of the stairs. You

167

are five feet apart, separated by the width of the stairs.

You withdraw the gun and crouch below the stairs. Laying down, you extend to the bottom step. You risk a quick look. Seeing nothing, you stretch your gun hand along the bottom step and work hard to control your breathing. Unless he pokes his head out, he can't see you. That's what you wait for.

Time passes with a slowness that leaves you weary. Every nerve in your body is taut and the strain takes a toll on your concentration and energy. You regain your focus as you hear something scraping, like material being dragged across a floor. You exhale in a long slow blow and increase the pressure on the trigger.

Along the floor directly across from you, you see a shock of hair. Then a forehead emerges in slow, steady progression. By the time the eyes break cover, you've got him. The explosion of the bullet startles you, even though you pulled the trigger. The other man's head rocks and sightless eyes stare back at you.

You lower your head to the floor, feeling the tension flow out of you. Your entire body slackens. You snap your head up some time later. You had fallen asleep. How strange.

You get up, search the man's pockets, finding a spare magazine and the van keys, then drag his body outside. You leave it more than a hundred yards behind the house. You feel no sense of satisfaction; just simple relief it's over. You head back to the house, thinking you still have a lot to do.

Go to Chapter 4 Page 139

3B3) The van has been gone for five minutes. You run upstairs to the front bedroom to get a better vantage point. If the man is lurking somewhere, you'll be able to see him from there.

You move the curtain back a fraction to look down at the street in front of the house. Nothing. You open the curtain wider and look to both sides. The van is not in sight. Somewhat relieved but still wanting to make sure it's gone, you go to your bedroom and dig through your closet until you find your binoculars. Standing in full view in the window, you scan the surrounding houses. From your higher perch, you can see much farther now. The houses block much of your view of the street. You can't see if he's parked and using a house for cover, but if he tries to approach the house either in the van or on foot, you'll see him.

You study the area for several minutes before deciding to check the back of the house. You enter your son's bedroom and scan the back. There are houses to the left and right, but behind is nothing but woods, and beyond that, only farmland. If someone were to approach from that direction, they could conceivably get within thirty yards of the house unseen—if they were good.

You do a slow pan of the tree line and are satisfied no one is there. You are about to turn away and check the front again, when movement from deeper in the woods catches your eye. You focus the glasses on the area in question, but see nothing out of the ordinary.

Then, a face peeks out from around a tree. You duck and let the curtain fall. Did he see you? Part of you hopes he did; then maybe he'll turn around and leave you alone. But that would only mean you'd have to deal with him another day, when you might not have the advantage. No, it is better if you handle this now.

Concerned that if he's looking, he'll see the curtain move, you run to the next bedroom in the back. You approach the window like you're sneaking up on it. Stepping to the side, you inch the curtain open and look without the glasses. From this angle, the tree hides the man from you.

Using the glasses, you do another scan, but he is no longer in view. *Damn! Where is he?* You know he's out there somewhere. Perhaps he saw you at the other window and left.

A sound near the house like something had fallen or was dropped draws your attention. You stand and press your head to the window. There's a bent leg.

Son of a bitch! He's on the deck—and it looks like he's trying to pick the lock.

You think fast. The window. You unlock the window and try to lift it. It sticks. You can't remember the last time it was opened, if ever. You wiggle it from side to side, thinking that might help break it free, but a second attempt results in the end of your efforts.

You tip toe to the other window in the room. It is farther away, but may offer a better shot. Unlocking and lifting that one has the desired result. The window glides upward with only a faint scraping sound.

The screen is dirty from years of wind-blown dust and dirt. Pushing your head against the screen gives you a better view. You see the man's back as he continues working on the lock.

Pressing in on the two latches, you lift the screen. It makes more noise than the window did. You see the man pause and look around, and then he looks up. He arches backward to see the windows above him, but he never looks in your direction.

The screen is only four inches high. You'll need more room to get off an accurate shot. You cock the hammer and set the gun down on the floor. Kneeling, you press the latches inward again and lift. The screen rises, scraping the tracks. The man hears it and stands up. He turns toward the noise and you reach for the gun. You have a space of about eight inches to use now. You'd like more room, but you have to make do.

You extend your gun hand out the window then turn your head as you squeeze it out. You get it far enough to see the man at the same moment he spots you. He reaches for his weapon as he turns to run for the side of the house. You trigger a fast shot and miss.

Without looking back, he extends his arm behind him and fires three quick shots. None come close, but you flinch and pull back long enough to allow him to get to safety. You can't see him, but guess he's running for the street.

You run for the front bedroom, yank the curtains aside and lift the window. He emerges from between the houses, gun pointed upward and runs across the neighbor's front yard. You don't bother with lifting the screen. You press the barrel against it and fire. You miss, but the hole you created allows you to push the barrel through.

Leading your target, you trigger continuous shots until, by some miracle, one strikes him and he tumbles into the street. You watch, open-mouthed for a moment, and see him trying to get to his feet.

You think about taking another shot, but know you were lucky to have hit him once from there. You run for the stairs. Leaping the last three, you land, tear open the front door and burst out.

The other man is hobbling down the street, dragging his left leg. You close the distance and raise your gun. There's no way you're gonna hit him on the run, so you save your bullets and get closer. He hears you and turns. He lifts the gun and you fire. Still running, you keep up a barrage of bullets without thinking about how stupid your actions are. A bloom of red appears on the man's chest. He staggers backward and lifts his gun again.

You keep pulling the trigger, but the slide locks back. You stare at the gun for a second in disbelief, but for some inexplicable reason you are still running toward the shooter.

He is having trouble keeping his balance. He aims the gun and pulls the trigger. The bullet whistles past your head. He wobbles backward from the gun's kick and tries to aim again. Before he can shoot again, you raise the gun and throw it at him. It strikes him in the chest and knocks him backward. Already off balance, he falls, hitting his head on the cement. The gun goes flying and he curls into a ball, holding his head.

You are next to him two steps later and bend over, hands on knees, trying to catch your breath.

He rolls onto his back, looks up and reaches a hand toward you. He gasps and says, "Can you help me?'

You look at him and shake your head. "No." You don't say it to be cruel, although he may think otherwise. But from the location of the wound, you know you have no skill to save him. The pain you would cause trying to extract the bullet would be worse than the death he faces.

You pick up his gun, then search his pockets, finding a spare magazine and the van keys. Squatting next to him, you say, "Sorry. There's nothing I can do."

He nods and closes his eyes.

"Is there anyone you want me to tell?"

He snorts what sounds like a wet laugh and shakes his head.

"There's no one left to tell."

You think about that for a second. "Well, you were left. It didn't have to be this way. We could've been allies."

"That's naive. It's everyone for themselves now." He coughs and a spray of blood dots his face.

"Yeah, but then you wouldn't be lying here now. We'd be cracking warm beers and talking about how we were gonna survive."

He says nothing, and as the light begins to dim in his eyes, you stand and walk home.

Go to Chapter 4 Page 177

Chapter 4

You sit in the family room and watch the woman sleep. *Will she stay? Will she fight? Will she try to kill you?* These questions and many others bounce around your head. You'll give her the chance to stay, to be a partner, but you will not force her. If she wants to go, so be it, but you will remind her about what happened to her friend when he tried to rob you.

You get up and open a bag of chips. It's not the best meal—you certainly have much more to choose from, but you don't want to leave her long enough to go downstairs, so chips and beer will do for now.

You finish the beer and fold over the chips bag, taking it back to the kitchen. When you return, the woman's eyes are open and she's taking in the surroundings. It takes a moment for the memories to come back. When they do, she jolts to a sitting position and eyes you warily.

* * *

Keeping a soft tone, you say, "You have nothing to fear from me, as long as you aren't here to harm me. You are welcome to stay as long as you are willing to work. If not, you are free to go. Just please, don't come back. I don't want to have to kill you too."

She doesn't speak, but her eyes are darting, searching for and weighting her chances of escape.

Understanding this, you back away and give her an open route to the door. She moves with tentative steps, not sure if it's a trick.

She pauses to look at you.

"Really? I can go? You won't stop me?"

"No. You are free. I don't know how you worked it with the other guy, but I won't hold you against your will."

She moves into the kitchen and toward the patio door, her eyes never leaving him. She stops. "Just so you know, I wasn't with him."

You nod. "Then you are welcome here."

She looks outside, then back at you. She sucks in her lower lip and gnaws at it. Tears well in her eyes. "I'm afraid."

"Of which? Staying or going?'

"Both."

"Then stay for a while. If you like it, fine. If not go. Just don't ever plan on stealing from me. If you can keep from doing that, we'll get along fine."

Her body trembles under the weight of indecision. You don't want to force her. "Take as long as you want to make up your mind, but I have a lot of work to do." You walk toward the kitchen and she backs up, fearful. You get within three steps of her and she cowers, but then you turn toward the garage. You grab a bag from the van and haul it in. When you come back, she's standing in the outside doorway, still unsure.

"If you decide to stay, I could use some help putting this stuff away. You'll get a meal when were done—and a safe place to sleep for the night." You go down stairs. She is still there when you return to the kitchen. You think she'll stay. She needs time.

You finish unloading the van and drop off the last bag in the basement. She's still ready to run.

"My name's (your name or) Larry." You wait but she doesn't speak. "Okay. 'Hey you' it is. I'm going to find this guy's van and see what he has. You're welcome to stay, but remember what I said about stealing. If you want to make yourself useful, go downstairs and begin putting away the items I just brought in. The shelves should be self-explanatory. If we work together, we'll get done faster and can eat sooner."

You go out the front door and hope you made the right decision.

It takes ten minutes to locate the van. When you get inside, you look through it and find he had been collecting, too. His van isn't as full as yours, but there's enough there to make the extra work worthwhile. You start it up and park it in the driveway.

He was using plastic tubs to carry his goods. You pick one up and go the door. *What will you find on the other side?* You push the door open, and for a moment feel disappointed when you don't see her. Then you hear something in the basement. You smile. Maybe she's decided to stay.

You carry the tub downstairs and see her busy stacking cans. She pauses upon seeing you. For a second fear flickers across her face. She glances at the stairs, perhaps wondering if she made a mistake, then it vanishes.

"Claire." She puts a can on the shelf. "My name's Claire."

Awesome!

"Nice to meet you, Claire. I've got four more tubs to carry in, then we can eat. See anything you like?"

"Oh yeah."

You laugh and go back out for the next load.

Finished, you allow her to pick out what you'll be having for dinner. To your surprise and delight, she chooses a can of beef stew. You smile. "Good choice. Grab another one, would you, please?"

She picks up another can and brings them to you. She looks nervous, but licks her lips in anticipation. The gesture makes you laugh.

She glances at you, then away. "Do we eat it cold?"

"We can, but let's not. Come on. I'll show you."

You go upstairs and grab a pot and a can opener, then go out to the deck and ignite the grill's side burner. You open the cans and dump them in the pot on the burner.

***

Claire says, "Your family?"

You look at her, then to the mounds of dirt where she nods. Sadness floods back. "Yeah."

"Sorry." The silence stretches before she says, "At least you know where they are. I have no idea where my family is."

"That would be hard, but at least you can still hope they're alive."

"Yeah. But sometimes I think the not knowing is worse than ..." she gestures with her head toward the graves.

"No," you say. "It's really not."

Neither of you speak again. You go inside and get two bowls, two forks and two bottles of water. You portion the food and hand her a bowl and a fork, then you both sit on the deck to eat. The silence goes on long after you finish. After a while, you take the bowls and forks inside and wipe them clean with a dampened paper towel.

"Well, I'm going to bed. You can sleep here, or there's three other bedrooms upstairs. Up to you. Good night."

You turn to go, and she says, "Thank you."

"No problem. Hopefully I'll see you in the morning."

You get no response, but you don't expect to. If she's there in the morning, great. If not, oh well. It was nice to have someone to talk to for a while. You fall sleep dreaming about your spouse.

Go to Chapter 5 Page 178

Chapter 4

You empty your van and go out to find the other one. It is parked two blocks away. Inside, you discover the same basic items you've been collecting. The van is half full. Unlike your plastic bags, he was hauling his loads in large plastic tubs.

You park in your driveway and unload, keeping alert for anyone else who might be in the area. As you work, you think about the woman. Could you have done anything different that might have saved her? Probably, but you have no idea what it would have been. It's a shame. It would've been nice to have someone around to talk to.

Your thoughts turn to the boy. He said he was going to stop by again today, but he didn't. You hope he's all right and make a mental note to look for him tomorrow.

Finished, you drive the van four blocks away and walk home. You eat a ham and cheese sandwich and an apple and a banana. The ham is a bit slimy. You decide it will have to be pitched. The fruit, too, is showing signs of age, but for the moment, it is still edible. You're determined to eat what you can for as long as you can, knowing that it will soon be impossible to find fresh fruit and vegetables.

You are groggy in the morning. Coffee sounds good. You pour two bottles of water into a pot and bring it to a boil on the grill's side burner. Then, you place a filter and coffee into the coffee maker. You pour the hot water over the grounds. The aroma hits you in an instant, and you inhale deeply. As the final drops fall, you take down a cup from a cabinet and fill it.

Wrapping both hands around the cup, you lift it to your nose. Close your eyes and breathe it in. "Ahh!"

"Can I have a cup?"

The voice startles you. Coffee sloshes everywhere, splashing on the countertop and over your hands. Scalded, you cry out while reaching for your gun, but realize you forgot to bring with you.

You turn and see the boy standing there a hand over his mouth muffling a laugh.

"Sorry. I didn't mean to scare you."

You're angry and your hands burns. You set your cup down and wipe your hand on your pants. "What the hell! Do you know how much I was looking forward to relaxing with a cup of coffee?"

"Hey, I said I was sorry."

"Yeah." You grab a few paper towels and mop up the spill. You look up to see he is leaving. "Hey! Where you going?"

"I guess, back home."

You feel bad for yelling at him. "No, stay. Have some coffee."

"You sure? I don't want to tick you off any more than I already have."

"You just surprised me, that's all. Plus, the coffee is really hot." You look at your hand. A wide red welt is blooming. You reach up and get another mug, fill it and hand it to him.

"Do you have any cream or sugar?"

Your first thought is to say, *Do I look like a coffee shop?* but you swallow the words. "The sugar's over there," you point to a canister. "Obviously, there's no milk, but I might have some of those creamer packets around here."

Chapter 5

In the morning, you grab your gun and leave your room. You check the other three bedrooms before going downstairs. They are all empty and untouched. To your disappointment, the couch is vacant, too.

The patio door opens, surprising you. You crouch and raise your gun, ready to take down an intruder, when Claire enters, carrying two steaming mugs. She doesn't see you at first; she uses her foot to close the door.

You slide the gun into your pants at the small of your back and beam a smile. She smiles back as she walks toward you, offering one of the mugs.

"Hope you don't mind, but I made coffee."

"Mind? Heck, no. I'd love some."

She places her cup down on the kitchen table and sits. You do the same. You inhale the aroma and take a tentative sip. It is extremely hot. You set the mug down.

"I, ah, I'm happy you're still here."

"Surprised, too, I'll bet."

"Yeah, that, too. Are you going to stay?"

"It depends."

"On?"

"A lot of things. I don't know you. I've met two people so far since all the deaths occurred. One tried to kill me. I guess it depends on what you want from me."

"Companionship. An ally. A partner. Someone to talk to and share the burdens of this new world with. I'll respect you. You'll be safe here."

She nods. "We'll see. Let's play it day by day. Okay?"

"Sure. Works for me."

You pick up the mug and try another sip. It is only slightly cooler, but you drink anyway. It burns all the way down.

"Well, let me explain my routine to you. I go out each day and search about ten houses, taking anything that might be of use to me. Then, I bring it all back and sort it on the shelves in the basement. So far, that's been the extent of my days. I want to get as much as possible from the houses as possible, before more scavengers come like yesterday."

"And what happens if they do and find your hoard? Won't they want to take it from you?"

"I'm sure some will try. All the more reason to develop an ally."

"But staying here with you might put me in danger."

"Being anywhere might put you in danger."

"True."

"Hey, like I said, it's up to you. Would you like to come with me on my run today? I could use the help."

"I'm not sure. Let me think about it."

"Okay, but let me say this—and I don't mean it to be insulting. If you don't come with me, I can't leave you here."

That puzzles her for the moment, then her eyes light, first with understanding, then with anger. You speak to head off a verbal confrontation.

"Look, let's be honest. If I leave you here, what's to stop you from stealing everything? Until you're ready to commit to a partnership, I'd be a fool to let you stay here alone."

"I could be here to protect your stash."

"True, and maybe someday it will come to that, but for now, until we get to know each other and feel comfortable, that's how it has to be. Come with me. We can clear more houses faster if we work together, instead of being rivals."

"And what if after we finish this neighborhood, I want to take my portion and leave?"

You mull that over. "I can't and won't hold you against your will. If you're not happy here, you can go, and yes, you can take what belongs to you. I won't stop you."

"Well, we'll see. But yes, I'll go with you today."

You lift your mug and drink while watching her over the rim. Is having her here a blessing or a curse? You'll have to keep an eye on her.

***

You gather your things and go to the garage. As you drive away, you explain your process. You show her the plat map and which houses you've been through. Then you show her where you plan on starting.

"Do you think that man has a stash here, too?"

"It's a possibility. Guess we'll find out."

You stop at your first house. Once inside, you say, "You do upstairs. Take anything you think might be useful. Especially medicines and first aid supplies."

"Okay."

She goes upstairs while you start on the kitchen. She finishes well before you do, so you send her into the basement. You are in the garage when she joins you.

"Okay, start lugging bags to the van." You hand her the keys, hoping you haven't made a mistake. While she's loading, you run upstairs to make sure you haven't missed anything. On the floor in a closet, you find a gray gun box. You open it—empty. You wonder if it was already gone, or if Claire took it. The hairs raise on the back of your neck. You will have to watch her closely.

Over the next few hours, you finish six houses. No doubt, having an extra person makes the job go much faster. You take a break. You both go through the bags and find something to eat and drink. While you rest, you say, "So, do you have any questions?"

She munches on a chocolate granola bar and shakes her head. "No, I think it's all logical." She sprays some crumbs.

"Yeah, pretty much. Did you find anything unusual?"

Her brows knit. She cocks her head to the side. "Unusual? Like what?"

"I don't know. Different. People often keep strange things around that only they know about."

"You mean like dildos and sex toys?"

You laugh. "Well yeah, that would be unusual. But not just that. Hidden stuff. Money, gold bars, dominatrix costumes…weapons."

You try not to eye her with suspicion, but she catches you.

"You found the box, didn't you?"

You nod.

"Look, I'm not going to shoot you. I'm also not going to give it to you. You have a gun. I should have one, too. I want to feel protected and not have to rely on you."

You nod again. That seems to annoy her.

"I promise I'm not going to shoot you. But, well, I also don't know you, and I guess I want to be sure. Having the gun makes us more even."

"No problem. But know this: I don't know you, either. We're having trust issues. Maybe they'll go away; maybe they'll get worse. But if I see you aim that gun at me, I will kill you."

She tenses and goes pale.

"I'm not trying to scare you or threaten you. I'm just telling you how it is. I pray it never comes to that. We understood?"

She swallows hard and nods.

"Okay. Let's get back to work."

You clear another five houses and are running out of room in the van, as well as out of energy. You still have at least two more hours of daylight.

"What do you want to do? Go home and unload or keep going?"

"I'm really tired, but it's still early. I hate to waste the time. Let's do two more."

"Okay, but I think we're gonna have trouble getting much more inside."

"Why don't we take another car?"

"Good idea. The next house has an SUV in the driveway. Hopefully, the keys are inside."

You break in and are greeted by the foul smell of death. You shrink back from the door. The odor hits Claire, and she gags and doubles over.

"Let's skip this one," she says.

You are inclined to agree, but you hate to waste what might be in there. You take off your shirt and press it to your nose. The smell of your sweaty shirt is almost as bad as that of the decaying bodies. You inhale a deep breath, away from the fabric, press it against your nose, and rush inside. Bodies are everywhere. There must be ten of them. You step over them and into the kitchen.

As fast as you can, you sweep entire shelves into the bag, but to do so, you have to put the shirt down. You feel like you're going to explode. The bag bounces over the bodies as you head for the door. You get outside just as you can no longer hold your breath.

You collapse on all fours and suck in fresh air.

"Was it worth it?"

You try to speak, but cough instead.

She looks through the bag and moves her head from side to side, as if to say *maybe so; maybe not.*

"Well," you say when you can talk, "should I go back in?"

"Hey, that's up to you. There's a lot of the same things we already have, but I guess you can never have too much."

You stand, gather your strength and resolve and draw in the deepest breath you can. Taking a fresh bag, you grab your shirt and tuck it into your pocket then move to the pantry. There's enough room to stand inside, so you press in and close the door. It helps block some of the stench. Enough that you can take shallow breaths.

The owners must have gone shopping before they died. The pantry is full. You fill a bag and find a box of garbage bags on the floor. You fill six bags, then taking a deep breath, exit, dragging two bags behind you.

"The pantry was full. I've got four more bags to get."

"Do you want me to help?" But by her expression, you can tell she doesn't really want to go inside.

"No, I'll do it. No sense both of us choking. It'll take two more trips. Why don't you start taking these out front? I'm not sure about finding a key for the SUV."

"I'll do what I can."

You put your shirt on and run back in. By the time you get the next two bags out, she's gone. You feel a twinge of anxiety. Will she be there when you get the last two bags out or will she have driven off? She'd have to know you'd go after her; that when you find her, she'll be dead. The anger builds as you go back for the last two bags.

On the deck, you don't wait until you get your breath back. You need to know if she's gone. You race around the house, struggling for breath, but the stench of death has permeated your nostrils. You round the corner and your fears are realized. The van is gone. Do you:

5A) get a car and follow her? Page 185

5B) get a car, load what you have, and go home? Page 193

5C) find another large vehicle and continue collecting? Page 196

5A) "Damn!" you shout. You walk down the driveway and look both ways. She couldn't have gone far. There are only two ways out of the subdivision. If she stayed in the neighborhood, she'd know you'd get to her eventually. Maybe she felt confident that she could defend herself with her newfound weapon. Well, she thought wrong.

You run back inside the house and search the pockets of the corpses. You find two sets of keys and run back out. You press the fobs. Neither one is for the SUV, but a Lexus parked on the street beeps at you. You sprint for it. The car starts and you drive for the south exit to the subdivision. If she's leaving the area, you guess she would choose the path you think to be least likely.

You race the engine to the exit. It ends in a T-intersection. You choose right and head to the main road that runs North-South. You pull out and look both ways. *Wait! Is that her?*

To the right at the edge of your sight, something is moving. It is the only thing you see, so you turn that way and push the pedal down. Whatever is no longer in sight. Did she turn or was she just around a bend?

You pound on the steering wheel, seeing the road through a red veil. Reaching behind you, you pull the gun out and set it on the passenger seat. You lean forward, as if that will increase your speed. Houses are a blur. You take a curve in the road too fast and almost crash into a tree. Forced to slow, you regain the road. In the distance, you spy a dot on the horizon. It's a vehicle and you strain to identify it, but it's still too far away.

It disappears again, and a minute later, you're closer and you swear you see it. It is the van. You're sure now. You will catch her, and she will pay. Over the next two minutes, you close the gap. After you lose sight of the van around a bend, you hit a long stretch of straight road and find it is the van is gone.

"No! It can't be."

You slow your speed, searching for anyplace it might have turned off. Several houses sit well off the road with long driveways leading to them, but no van. You drive farther, but still nothing. Then, blocked from view by low-hanging branches, you see a green sign for a road that only goes to the right. You take it. It's a dirt road, and you see the dust still settling from a vehicle that has recently passed. You press on.

The condition of the road prevents high speeds, but you figure you can follow the settling dust cloud. Besides, the van won't handle the road as well as the Lexus did. It would also be moving slow.

You drive about a half mile, and the air is suddenly clear. You stop and look left and right. Only a wide-open field to the left. On the right, you see an old farmhouse in the distance. The trail of dust leads in that direction.

You put the car in reverse and back up until you find the driveway hidden between a long row of trees and shrubs. Do you:

5A1) drive up the driveway? Page 187

5A2) park and walk up? Page 190

5A3) decide it is not worth the effort or the risk and go home? Page 192

5A1) You aim the car up the driveway and go slow. You don't want to announce your presence by kicking up more dust. Hopefully, the dust cloud Claire created will still be hanging in the air to help cover your approach. You keep going until you see the van and part of the house. You hesitate, but decide to go all the way. She is not going to stop you from getting your stuff back.

You stop beside the van, pick up your gun, and get out. No sooner does your foot touch the ground, then gunshots erupt. The sound is deeper than that of a hand gun. Bullets from a high-powered rifle tear through the car. Glass shatters; a tire deflates.

You duck and jump behind the van for cover. Either Claire is a good shot, or someone else is there.

The shooting ceases. A male voice shouts out. "Why are you here?"

"You took my van."

"It's our van now."

A second male voice from somewhere else says, "Best you turn around and forget about your van. Don't want to kill you, but ain't opposed to it, either."

Shit! If Claire was with them, it is three against one. The van no longer seems important. Besides, you can deal with them at a later time. The problem is, Claire knows where you live and what you have. Will they come for it? Of course, they will. They stole the van, why wouldn't they clean out the house?

"Okay. I'm going. Don't shoot." You turn toward the car and see the flat. "You shot out my tire. I can't go."

"Guess you'll have to walk, then," the first man says. His voice sounds louder; closer. They are closing in on your position. If you don't move, you'll be dead. You move to the van's passenger door and open it. The seat where Claire sat is empty. You step in and pull the door closed, but don't shut it tight. You squeeze into the wheel well, gun up and wait.

The crunch of a footstep on gravel sounds close. If they know where you are, you're dead. You pull the hammer back. It makes a loud click inside the van. You cringe.

Outside the van, you hear a whispered, "Where'd he go?"

Silence. Then, the van door swings open, and in your surprise and fear you remember to pull the trigger. The man flies backward, his rifle discharging into the air.

"You son of a bitch."

You get up and dive across to the driver's seat. You open the door and fall out head first as a barrage of bullets rip through the van. You drop toward the ground, check your fall with your hands and let your legs flop. You roll over and try to get to your feet, but stumble. The shooting has stopped. You hear a man scream in rage, followed by running footsteps.

You get to your knees as a man carrying a rifle runs around the front of the van. You pull the trigger three times before he can bring his rifle on target. He is blown backward to the ground. His body twitches. You hear a raspy intake of breath…then a low gurgle…then nothing.

You spin, searching for another target. You see none. *Where's Claire?* Anger replaces your fear. She must pay.

Something hits against the interior wall of the van. Curious, you move toward the rear doors. It sounds as if someone is inside, trying to get out. You put your hand on the door and are about to open it, when you remember what you did to the first shooter. You step to the side.

Whipping the door open, you brace for the ambush shots, but none come. You risk a peek and snap your head back. Your quick glance showed you the bags were all still piled, but there was something else. You sneak another look. It's Claire. She's on her back, gagged and bound, covered by bags.

Your anger bleeds off, leaving you with a hollow feeling in the pit of your stomach. You are relieved to find she did not steal the van, but you'd worked up such a powerful need for revenge, that you feel let down at having no outlet for it.

You drag her forward and cut her bonds. She throws her arms around you and cries. You place an arm around her to lend comfort as you watch the house for other assailants.

Once Claire settles down, she explains, "I shoved the first bags into the van. When I closed the doors, they were standing there. I was hit on the head with the butt of a rifle. When I came to, I was tied up and in the van. I was so scared. Oh my God. What would they have done if you never found me?" She shudders, thinking of her fate, and cries again.

After a few minutes, you each pick up a rifle and go to the house. Though the outside looks junky, with rusted cars and farm equipment littering the yard, the inside is immaculate. There are several things you can use, but decide to leave everything except for the rifles and a box of ammo.

You drive back in silence, each lost in your own thoughts.

Epilogue Page 198

5A2) You maneuver the car so it blocks the driveway. You don't want her to. Then, gun in hand, you advance on the farmhouse. The driveway is at least a quarter-mile long. You keep moving until you see the back of the van. The rear doors are open. You squat and listen.

You hear a muffled scream that sounds like a woman's. That confuses you; if Claire stole the van, why would she be screaming? You move to the end of the trees, giving you a good line of sight to the yard and front of the house. The ground is littered with rusted cars, trucks, and farm equipment. Two men are climbing the front porch steps, carrying the bound and gagged body of Claire.

You are relieved to know she didn't steal the van and angry at the two men. While they are occupied with Claire, you move closer. You can't let them get her into the house where they can barricade the door.

One of the men has a rifle strung over his back. If the second man has a weapon, you don't see it. You reach the sidewalk in front of the steps, and the man nearest the door spots you. He calls out a warning. The man with his back to you spins, dropping Claire's feet. He reaches for the rifle and you call out, "Don't," but whether he heard makes no difference. As the rifle slides from his shoulder into his hands, you stop and fire. The bullet hits him high on the left side, spinning him around and down.

The second man has also dropped Claire. He opens the door and tries to enter, but you fire until you see him drop face first across the threshold.

You run up the steps and crouch next to Claire. Her bound hands are trying to cover her head. She curls into a ball. You yank the gag out, and she cries. "My head. The bastards dropped me on my head."

You cut her hands and legs loose and let her recover while you make sure no one else is left to shoot at you. You are amazed by how clean the interior of the house is. You do a quick run through, noting how much it looks like a prepper's hideout.

You leave everything but a box of ammo for the rifle. Outside, you pick up the rifle and help Claire to her feet and into the van.

"Do you feel all right to drive?"

"Not really. I have an awful headache."

Reaching the end of the driveway, you back the Lexus out of the driveway and head home.

Epilogue Page 199

5A3) Screw that. You came this far. You're gonna make her pay. Go back and choose another option.

5B) You have no way of knowing where she went. Though raging inside, chasing her was a waste of time. You go back inside, and after searching several bodies, find two sets of keys. You drag the remaining bags to the street and press the fobs. A Lexus beeps. You're glad; you've always wanted to drive one of those. You load the bags and drive home.

You spend some time putting your haul away, trying not to think about the way Claire had stabbed you in the back. That's what you get for trusting. Never again.

You are so upset, you can't bring yourself to go out again. You nibble at some junk food and go to bed early. You will have to put it all behind you and start over again in the morning, alone. Sunrise comes early. You drive to where you left off and start your routine. The Lexus proves too small at the first house. You will have to find a larger vehicle. You are forced to go home to unload. As you drive back to your next target house, you spy the van parked in the street with the motor running. You pull over and watch.

You can't believe she has the nerve to come back. Heat rises from your stomach and flushes your cheeks. She is gonna pay, and she is gonna tell you where she took your stuff.

The van moves forward. It hesitates at the next house, the one you just finished, then pulls up the driveway. Two men get out, but no Claire. Maybe she's the getaway driver. Both men are carrying rifles. One is holding a large hammer. They move to the front of the house. The one with the hammer hands his rifle to the second man, and with a powerful swing, blasts the door from its frame.

You wait until they get inside, then get out and run for the van. You form a plan. If she's inside with the keys, you'll throw her out, get in and drive away. You want to shoot her, but a gun blast might draw the armed men.

You close in on the side of the van and take an angle clear from the mirror's view. You duck and walk to the passenger door, then around the front of the van until you are even with the driver's door. You grab the handle, stand, pull and aim. As the door opens, you confront an empty seat. You step in and discover the van is empty and no one is hiding inside.

So, where the hell was Claire? Or, thinking perhaps you're mistaken, *what the hell happened to Claire?*

You turn to the house. Only those two men know for sure. You move to the side of the splintered front door and listen. They are loud, oblivious to how much noise they are making. One says, "Look at all this food."

"Oh yeah, we hit the motherlode."

You don't enter, fearing you will step on or kick part of the door. So, you wait. When they come out, they will have their hands full. It will be easier to get the drop on them. You back away to the corner of the house and wait.

Fifteen minutes later, one of the men comes out hauling a large box in both hands; his rifle slung over his shoulder. You let him get close to the van before you go for him. After a look through the open door, seeing his partner, you move fast, striking him on the back of the head with the gun. He drops and the box hits the ground and upends. Cans and packages scatter and roll, making a loud clatter. You run to the edge of the garage, out of sight from the front door, and prepare for the next one.

"Doobie, what happened? Hey man, you all right?"

Footsteps scrape on cement. He's coming down the walkway.

"Doobie?"

You spin out and he sees you. He swings his gun toward you as you fire. Both of you fire panic shots that go wide. You fire blindly as you run for the van, the rifle round pinging off the front bumper.

"You son of a bitch. I'm gonna kill you. You better not have hurt my brother."

You creep from the back end of the van to the driver's side. You spin around fast, drawing a bead, but he's not there. Fear grips your heart. You pivot toward the back of the van from where you just came and see the rifle barrel coming around the side. You aim and fire. The man walks right into your bullet. A look of surprise crosses his face. He drops to his butt, blinks a few times, then falls back with a moan.

Noise to your left draws your attention. You turn to see the first man scrambling to get his rifle.

"Don't. I'll shoot you, too."

The man hesitates, understanding the implications of your words.

He spits venomous words. "If you shot my brother, I'll kill you." The rifle hits his hands and you try to talk fast.

"I just want to know where the woman is. Tell me that, and I won't shoot."

He pauses again, then a sinister smile crosses his face. "Oh, was that your woman? She's good. I'm gonna go home and enjoy her again after I kill you."

His words ignite a rage like you've never felt before. You pull the trigger and watch his head explode.

You move to stand over him, your fury nowhere near sated. Where could she possibly be?

You turn your face to the sky and scream, "Claire!"

Epilogue Page 201

5C) With no idea where to begin looking, you give up. You sit on the front porch for a while to regroup your thoughts and bottle your anger. You vow to find her. And when you do, she will pay for her betrayal.

Releasing a deep sigh, you get up and go in search of a new vehicle. You find a Suburban three houses down. The keys are lying on the floor next to their deceased owner. After starting the large SUV, you back down the driveway and return to the house where the van was parked.

As you load your new ride, you shake off another wave of anger, thinking about all the supplies you lost. "Oh well, nothing I can do about it now."

You drive to the next house and start over. It's a shame; you liked having someone to talk to. But even if you find someone else, how will you ever be able to trust again?

You work until dark, and by the end of the night, with everything in its place on the basement shelves, you feel good about recouping. You open a bottle of Pinot Noir and heat up a can of clam chowder, both part of your recent haul.

You eat and finish two glasses of wine. The day's work, coupled with the food and wine, leave you so tired that you nod off in your seat on the deck. You snap awake at the sound of someone stomping up the deck.

You see a form materialize before you and spring to your feet. Gun in hand you, face the intruder.

"Whoa! Don't shoot. It's me. Andy."

You relax a fraction. "Andy? What are you doing here so late? You startled me and almost got shot."

"S-sorry. I came by earlier, but you were gone."

You allow your heart rate to decline a few beats before saying, "So, why are you here?"

"I, ah, I thought about what you said, you know, about working together, and decided it was a good idea. So, here I am."

A nervous silence ensues. After Claire's betrayal, you're not sure you want to take another chance.

He rushes to say, "I brought all the stuff you bagged up. I figured if we are gonna team up, everything should be in one place."

You still don't speak.

"That's all right, isn't it?"

This is different from Claire. She brought nothing with her. She had nothing invested in staying. That should've been a red flag to you. You know better now. But Andy has brought all his possessions to add to your stash. Not to mention that he is only about twelve.

"Yeah, that's all right. Why don't you take the stuff into the basement and put everything where it belongs?"

Andy drags the two bags to the patio door.

"Are you hungry? I can fix you something."

"Ah, yeah, that'd be cool."

"Okay. Bring up what you want to eat and I'll heat it up."

He enters the house and you go into the kitchen to get another plate and utensils. It will be good to have someone to talk to, even if he is a kid. You won't give him your trust yet. He'll have to earn it. Nevertheless, you have a feeling it will work out.

Epilogue Page 203

Epilogue 5A1) Over the next week, with the two of you working together, you manage to finish the remaining houses. On the next to the last day, you discover the other man's hideout and strip it. He'd collected quite a bit. Over the elapsed time, you've gotten to know Claire. She's nice and a hard worker. Your friendship grows. It's nice to have someone to share the apocalypse with.

You reveal an idea that has been rattling around your mind ever since Claire's kidnapping.

"You know, once we're done collecting, there won't be anything to keep us here. We can move somewhere more remote and safer."

"Sounds like you've already got one in mind."

"Yep. I was thinking about that old farmhouse those idiots took you to. It's large and away from anything else. We can easily see anyone coming down the road. We could even plant some crops. Food isn't always gonna be easy to find. Besides, fresh is better than canned."

She thinks it over for a few minutes, then says, "Yeah, sounds like a plan."

Once you've been through every house, you begin hauling your supplies to the new location. It takes two full days to make the move.

You bury the bodies of the men next to two other fresh graves you find fifty yards from the house in a small split-rail enclosure under a willow.

Claire takes over setting up the kitchen and putting away the food and supplies, while you go about moving all the rusted machines into a small copse of trees a hundred yards to the east.

After a while, you settle into a routine. You still do a daily collection, but only in the morning. After lunch, you work the fields. It makes for a long day, but what else is there to do? You might have survived the apocalypse, but if you are going to continue to do so, it will take a lot of work.

But at least you're alive for the moment.

Epilogue 5A2) It takes several days for Claire to push her ordeal aside enough to want to get out of the house. You work together and clear more than half of the subdivision in a week.

One morning, you exit your house to find Andy sitting on the back deck. He has several garbage bags with him.

"Ah, hi, I, ah, didn't want to wake you, so I sat here until you got up."

"Okay. And why are you sitting here?"

"I've been giving what you said, you know, about working together, a lot of thought. I think it's a good idea. I can help you a lot and we ..."

Claire comes out. Her hair's a mess and she's wearing pajama bottoms and a t-shirt. Andy stops mid-sentence.

"Andy, this is Claire. She's staying here, too."

"Hi, Andy. Nice to meet you."

"Yeah, hi." He looks nervous. "Does that mean you don't need a partner anymore?"

You turn to Claire, "Andy was looking to move in and join the team."

"Oh, what a great idea."

"You mean it's okay if I stay?"

You say, "Of course. Take your things inside and pick a room. There's two left."

Claire says. "If you have any food items you want stored, let me know. I'll help you put it away."

"Okay." He drags the bags inside.

Claire smiles at you. "Wow! Aren't we a growing family?" She laughs and goes inside.

You stand at the grill and make coffee. Your eyes find the graves of your spouse and son. You say a prayer and think, *From one family to another—just like that.* You vow to do everything in your power to keep this one safe.

You pour the water over the grounds and make three cups. Placing them on the table, you sit, sip and smile.

Epilogue 5B) You comb the neighborhood, but don't find her. You give up and go home, too distraught to empty your day's collection. You sit on the deck with your face in your hands. All that anger, for nothing. She hasn't betrayed you after all. She'd been kidnapped. *God*, you pray, *let her be all right and let her get free.* Maybe if she does, she'll come back. It's all you can hope for. Thinking of her dying in some locked room with her hands tied is too much to bear.

You look at your family's graves and cry. The tears fall for a long time. A scraping sound from somewhere in the yard snaps you into a defensive attitude. You pull our gun, hoping for a confrontation. You want to punish someone, anyone, for what happened to Claire.

You strain to pierce the darkness. A shadow moves and you aim your gun at the center of it.

"Don't shoot. It's Andy."

You blink in rapid patterns as his words sink in. You battle against the rage, but manage to bring it under control.

"Step to where I can see you."

The scraping starts again.

"Stop! What's that noise?"

"I'm dragging those bags you packed."

It registers in a moment. The bags you collected at his house, before you knew he was living there.

"Okay. Come ahead."

Andy appears at the bottom of the stairs.

"What's all this?"

"I gave a lot of thought to what you said, you know, about teaming up, and decided that'd be a good thing. If it's still all right."

"Yeah. It's cool. Come on up."

Andy drags the bags up the stairs. They look torn and stretched, like they might not hold much longer.

"Put them inside. We can empty them tomorrow."

Andy drags them through the patio door and deposits them on the kitchen floor. He comes out and sits at the table.

"You hungry?"

"Yeah. I could eat."

"Yeah, I'll bet you can. You got anything in those bags worth eating?"

"Yeah."

"Well, go pick something out and I'll heat it up for you."

He brings back a can of ravioli with meat sauce.

While you heat the contents, you think about Claire and having a family again. You look back at Andy and vow to protect this one better.

You have a lot to learn about this dangerous new world, but having someone to share it with is half the battle. Do you:

    E1) decide to do whatever it takes to survive?

    E2) have any other choice?

End

Epilogue 5C) Andy learns quick, and over the next few weeks, you finish collecting from the entire neighborhood. You teach Andy how to drive and how to shoot. You teach him what to look for in necessities and protection. One day while Andy is in a house collecting, and you are rearranging the items in the back of the SUV to fit another bag. You step down and feel the cold metal of a gun press against the back of your head.

A man says, "Is there anyone else here?"

You swallow hard and shake your head. "No. I'm alone."

"Back out of there."

You do.

"Now kneel."

Again, you comply.

"Lock your fingers together behind your head." As you do that, the man glances through the Suburban's back door. "Nice haul. You did all this alone?"

"Yeah."

"Nice of you to do the work for me. Where are the keys?"

"My pocket."

You try to think about how to turn this to your advantage, but he says, "Take them out and toss them to me. And move with care."

You rethink your next move. Taking the keys out, you:

     E1) toss them to the side? Page 196

     E2) throw them hard at the man? Page 197

     E3) toss them to him? Page 199

E1) You take the keys and toss them to the side, and as he tracks them with his eyes, you get up and charge him. It's a desperate move, but you do it anyway. The man pulls the trigger twice as you come within two steps of him.

The bullets pound into your body like blows from a hammer. You fall, stunned, but surprisingly feel little pain. Is that a good thing or a bad thing?

Feet are next to your face. You strain to look up. He is looking down at you with a blank expression. "Dumb move." He aims the gun at your head and you close your eyes. You don't feel the last shot, but you do feel the weight that falls on you.

Opening your eyes, you see Andy through the dead man's legs. He is holding the gun you gave him in outstretched hands. *Good man, Andy.*

He rolls the body off you and kneels.

"What can I do?" he says. "Tell me. I don't know what to do."

"It's okay." The words are hard to push out. You feel weak. "Be strong. You can survive. Remember what I told you."

His eyes fill with tears.

"You'll be fine, son."

Your eyes close for the last time.

End

E2) You pull the keys out of your pocket and act like you're going to toss them to him. At the last second, you draw your arm back and throw them as hard as you can. The man shoots.

The bullet grazes your arm as you rise. The keys hit him in the arm holding the gun. You rush him as he triggers another round. This one impacts in your side and turns you, but you keep your legs churning. Before he can fire point-blank into your chest, you push his arm aside and tackle him.

The pain in your side is excruciating, but at least it means you're alive. You grapple for control of the gun, rolling over several times and exchanging the top position. He is stronger and angles the gun with slow but steady progress toward your face.

He knees you in the groin. You double over as all the air is expelled from your lungs. Your grip weakens enough and he twists the gun from your hand. He turns it on you, but before he can shoot, a bullet tears through his face, and he falls on top of you.

You panic and kick him away. You stand to see Andy there, holding the gun you gave him in outstretched and shaking hands. Tears fall as you approach and gently take the weapon from him.

He throws himself against you and sobs. It is traumatic for anyone to take a life, but especially for a twelve-year old. *He'll get over it*, you think; perhaps he'll have to do it again someday. It's good to know that he can kill if he must.

"Hey, you did good. You saved my life."

You let him cry for a minute before the burning in your side becomes too much.

"Andy, I need to get home. I've been shot and you need to help me take care of it."

He pulls back in alarm. The space gives you a chance to check the wound. "Good. It came out." You try to smile at him. "That means you won't have to learn how to be a doctor and perform surgery. You'll just have to be a nurse and help me clean, suture and bandage it. See what a good, well-rounded education the apocalypse is giving you?"

He drives home.

"You saved my life, Andy. Thank you."

He doesn't know what to say, but you're glad he decided to join you.

As you lie down for Andy to begin his work, you have an important decision to make. Do you:

      E2a) take shots of whiskey to deaden the pain?

      E2b) take shots of tequila to deaden the pain?

      E2c) bite on a stick?

E3) You take the keys out of your pocket and toss them to him.

"Good choice," he says with a smirk.

Keeping his gun trained on you, he backs to the driver's side of the SUV. He reaches the door and you try to decide if you should run or stay. If he was going to shoot you, wouldn't he have done it already? He still may, but why are you staying there, making it easy for him?

He reaches out and opens the door. This is the moment. As soon as he steps inside, you're going to move right, using the SUV for shielding.

He lifts his leg to get in and you push up and run behind the Suburban. A gunshot rings out, followed by silence. You're not sure which way to run. It all depends where the shooter is moving.

You stand to peek through the rear window, but the gunman is nowhere to be seen. Panic swelling within, you look left to right. You get ready to run as fast as you can, putting distance between yourself and the next bullet. The farther away you are and the more you move, the harder target you'll be, or at least, so he'd you'd seen on TV.

You take your first step when someone calls your name. Confused, you look back and see Andy standing at the front of the SUV with his gun out. Afraid for the boy, you yell, "Andy. Run!"

But he doesn't move.

"It's okay. I shot him. I think he's dead."

That stops you. You turn and walk back toward him. Moving around the vehicle, you see the body. You bend to check it and sure enough, the boy killed him. You look at Andy. He looks dazed. You slip an arm around his shoulders.

"It may not feel like it, but you did the right thing. He might've killed both of us. You didn't have a choice."

You look at him. He doesn't even blink as he stares at the body. You move him so it is out of his line of sight.

"You okay?"

He shrugs.

"You saved my life. It's all right to feel bad about killing someone, but when you have no other choice, it's justified. It was his decision to rob me at gunpoint. He could've joined us or asked for help. Instead, he chose to steal with a gun in his hand.

"Believe me, if the roles were reversed, I would've shot him, too. Once you process this and put it in the proper perspective, you'll understand you did the only thing possible, given the situation. Let's go home."

Andy is quiet the rest of the night. You eat in silence and let him be while you empty the SUV. In the morning, he seems more like himself. He sips coffee while you fix breakfast. While you eat, he says, "So, what do we do today?"

You smile. "Well, we have a choice. We can:

E3a) go back and pick up where we left off."

E3b) leave the area and try someplace new."

E3c) go fishing."

His face lights up and you know what he's decided.

End

COLLECTION LIST

FOOD
Canned foods
Packaged foods
Dry beans
Dry pasta & rice
Granola Bars

LARGE ITEMS
Propane tanks
Gasoline & gas cans
Car battery charger
Short wave radio
Walkie-Talkies

DRINKS
Bottled water
Fruit drinks
Canned drinks
Beer

MEDICAL
Bandages
Disinfectants
Antibacterial ointment
Peroxide
Antibiotics
Epsom salts
Alcohol
Vinegar
Saline
Baking soda
Assorted meds & vitamins
Medical tape
Liquid bleach

WEAPONS
Guns
Ammo
Knives
Bows & arrows

10011476R00116

Made in the USA
Lexington, KY
22 September 2018